JAMILA GAVIN

When I am asked if the Surya trilogy is autobiographical, the answer is yes and no. Yes, that I couldn't have written it had I not been born in India into the period leading up to the Second World War, independence and partition; yes, that as a child I lived both in a palace in the Punjab and in a drab flat in a war-damaged London street; yes, that music, sea voyages, schools, friends were all part of my rich Anglo-Indian experience. But no – in any accurate sense to do with the plot or events described in the books. Everything I experienced simply became material with which I could overlay a complete fantasy. As a child can turn a table into a house or two chairs into a train, I turned my life into a fiction in which any resemblance to characters living or dead is purely coincidental – as they say in the movies.

JAMILA GAVIN

Winner of the Whitbread Children's Award

The Track
of the
Wind

The third part of the Surya trilogy

mammoth

The poem on page 114 is by Mir Taqil Mir
translated by D. J. Matthews in 1995 in *Urdu Literature*,
published by Third World Foundation
copyright © 1995 D. J. Matthews
Every effort has been made to trace the copyright holder

First published in Great Britain 1997
by Egmont Children's Books Limited
Reissued 2001 by Egmont Children's Books Limited
a division of Egmont Holding Limited,
239 Kensington High Street, London W8 6SA

ISBN 0 7497 4742 0

A CIP catalogue record for this title is available from the British Library

Printed and bound in Great Britain by Cox and Wyman Ltd, Reading, Berkshire

Contents

By means of waking and sleeping, the Imperishable One brings to life this whole universe, moving and unmoving, and tirelessly destroys it. **Manu's Law**

Prologue

In this age of darkness
Men have become as dogs. **Rag Sarang**

A man came to Deri. The few people who glimpsed him on the way said he was a monster. He had been beaten till his bones were shattered and he had been so badly burned that his face was nothing but a smudge – with eyes that could not close, a nose reduced to two holes and a mouth which was merely a slit. He looked like a badly made rag doll. So he draped himself with a shawl – even when the sun was at its hottest – and wound the loose end of his turban round his face.

He came by foot – travelling alone. Invisibly.

He learned to be as unnoticed as a brown lizard against the brown earth. By day he merged perfectly into the background, by night he slept rough in fields and ditches, or in the

1

disused bungalows of departed Britishers. He walked for months and months, begging for food or getting the hospitality of gurudwaras on the way. At last, he came to his own land.

Day after day, he hung about in the fringes of the undergrowth watching the life of the village. He peered through his painful unshielded eyes at those who worked the soil beyond the sugar-cane fields. He took up residence within the ruins of the old palace by the lake, considered too haunted for people to frequent, and bided his time.

1 The letter

A cyclist was silhouetted against the brightening sky. His white dhoti billowed gently under a post office regulation khaki jacket. He hovered on the rim of the dyke, then plunged down into the shadow of the road. Out of sight for a while, he emerged back into the light, pedalling easily along the straight path towards the village. Jhoti was already running to meet him. 'Have you a letter for us?' she asked eagerly. 'Is it from England?'

'Huh, huh!' He waved the letter in the air, teasing her. 'It's not for you, mamaji – nor Govind, and it's not from England.'

'From where then, where?' cried Jhoti, bursting with curiosity.

The postman came to a stop and rested his feet on the ground. He brought the envelope close to his nose and examined it in a short-sighted sort of way. 'Singapore . . . Hmm . . . Burma. Now why should a certain person be getting a letter from the Royal Navy?' He questioned her with a cheeky smile and a tapping of his nose.

'What certain person?' exclaimed Jhoti, beginning to get annoyed and impatient. 'Give it here, Roshan, and stop fooling about.' She snatched it from him.

'It's for your daughter, Miss Marvinder Singh!' Roshan pre-empted her, knowing full well that Jhoti couldn't read. 'That's the third one I've brought for your daughter since she came back from England.'

'And so?' declared Jhoti. 'Oh, be off with you – you busybody.' Jhoti sped away to deliver the letter to Marvinder, who was crouched on her haunches in the kitchen, kneading chapatti dough and preparing food for the day.

'Is it from Kathleen? Or from Edith?' Jhoti asked, as Marvinder stared at the envelope. Without answering, Marvinder ran out to the pump to wash the sticky flour from her hands. Then, drying them hurriedly on the end of her veil, she excitedly took the letter from her mother.

Her mother peered over her daughter's shoulder at the squiggles on the paper, wishing that she could decipher them. 'Is it from the Chadwicks? But no, this one can't be. Roshan says it's from Singapore. Kathleen wouldn't be in Burma, would she?' Jhoti waited patiently as Marvinder skilfully prised open the envelope without ripping it. With arched fingers, she extricated a sheet of paper and began to read.

Jhoti sighed. How marvellous it was that Marvinder could

read and write and was so educated. Perhaps all the agonies of the past two years – the separation and terrible uncertainty brought about by war – had been worth it. For two years she had searched for her children, going all the way to Bombay, walking the streets, asking at the train station, the docks, the gatemen at the churches, if anyone had seen them or could tell her where they might be, and if they were alive or dead. But all in vain. Somehow, ill and heart-broken, she had made her way back to her ravaged village and crept into the jungle, not caring whether she lived or died.

But all the time, Jaspal and Marvinder had been in England with their father. They had been at English schools learning to read and write. They could have stayed on for ever. But they didn't. They came home to look for her.

Jhoti watched her daughter's face. 'Well?' she demanded, desperate to be included in the news. 'What's it all about? What is this place, Singapore? Where is it? Who do you know there?'

'It's from Kathleen's brother, Patrick,' said Marvinder. She looked up at her mother.

'Oh?' Jhoti was shocked. The shining in Marvinder's eyes was unmistakable. 'A boy is writing to you?' She looked around as if afraid that even such words would be compromising.

'Oh, Ma!' Marvinder laughed, trying to play down the implication. 'It's only Patrick – he's just a – ' She was going to say, just Kathleen's brother. But he wasn't just a brother, he was a man; he was eighteen; that's why he had been called up as a conscript in the British Royal Navy. Here in her village, most young men of his age were long married and were fathers already. 'He's written to me because he knew I wanted to collect stamps, and he was going to go all round the world with the navy and send me some from every place, that's all.' Breathless with the ease at which she had concocted a logical reason for the letter, Marvinder tried to divert her mother by showing her the stamps on the envelope. 'Look, Ma! Aren't they beautiful? I'm building up quite a collection. Kathleen and Edith both said they would write to me and send me stamps – and Dr Silbermann too. Now I have these! Aren't I lucky!'

Jhoti was dying to ask, what does it say? What is he like – this boy who is in the navy? Is he handsome? Do you feel for him? Did he ever touch you? But suddenly she didn't dare. The least said about this letter the better – especially in front of Govind.

'Put it away, daughter. Put it away. Your father would not like to know a boy has been writing to you. Here – shall I burn it?' Jhoti almost snatched it from her.

'No, Ma!' Marvinder recoiled in horror. She thrust the letter back into its envelope and pushed it into the waist of her salwaar pyjamas. 'It's mine. I'll keep it safe. Don't worry.'

Jhoti turned away feeling disturbed and anxious. She wanted to say, don't let your father know, but to advise such a thing would be disloyal. She knew she should take the letter and give it to Govind, but these days Govind had become so strict and austere, she was afraid of his reaction.

He was trying desperately to find a husband for Marvinder. But no family had yet made them any offers. He was afraid that her stay in England had made her too independent and different from the other village girls of her class. He wanted to tame her; make her submit. These days, he often lectured her and sometimes beat her. He disapproved of her writing and receiving letters. He disliked the way she spent so much time reading – in fact – devouring books as if she would be a scholar. Govind hated all this. It was as if he wanted to eradicate the past two years from her life, and make her the simple, innocent, dutiful daughter she would have been, had the world not turned upside down. If he knew about the letter . . . Jhoti's thoughts hung in the air. If he knew about the letter . . . She stood for a moment frowning as she imagined what he would do if he knew a boy was writing to his daughter, even though he was desperate for someone to present himself as a prospective husband.

Mother and daughter returned to their tasks in silence, grinding the spices, sifting the lentils and kneading the dough for chapattis. But all the time their minds were on the letter.

It was nearly midday before Marvinder was able to slip away on her own. She had only skimmed down Patrick's letter in the presence of her mother and was desperate to read it again.

This was the first time Patrick had written to her. The envelope had burned against her skin all morning as she had worked side by side with her mother. Every now and then she saw Jhoti glancing at her – her curiosity mingled with anxiety, and Marvinder would give her mother a reassuring smile.

Marvinder knew how her mother suffered more than she did when Govind raged at her and sometimes slapped her about for being distracted or lazy, or for not being exactly where he thought she should be at any given moment, or for not doing what he thought she should be doing then and there. Marvinder knew that her mother was torn between loyalty to her husband and a desire to protect her daughter. So, for her sake, Marvinder quelled the rebellious feelings which would well up inside her.

But she was always looking for ways to be by herself, where she could write to Kathleen or read some of the books she had found abandoned in the old missionary bungalows. Most of all, she needed somewhere to play her violin. It wasn't easy, for there were barely any hours in the day which weren't taken up with fetching and carrying and preparing food, and cooking and washing. Then there was the work in the fields – especially at harvest time, when every man, woman and child had to pull their weight, scything, cutting and gathering up.

But when the sun was at its zenith and the heat of the day too much, that was when Marvinder could escape unnoticed and go to the palace.

The palace had been built by a Mogul prince hundreds of years ago. It had once had a hundred rooms and stables for a hundred horses and tethering for two dozen elephants. Warriors had patrolled the ramparts and princes practised archery in the mango groves. In the cool of late afternoons, as the blood-red sun plunged downwards, princesses had been rowed up and down the lake, trailing their fingers in the water and watching the movement of fishes beneath the green silky surface. Not it was abandoned; forgotten; its rajahs defeated in battle, its riches pillaged. It looked like nothing but a mouldering wedding cake being slowly consumed by wind and rain and vermin. Grass and weeds, wild flowers and thin saplings sprouted from between the cracks, as if they too would swallow up the great grey stones, and no one would remember that, once, those rajahs and princes of unimaginable wealth and power had ruled this land.

Marvinder entered through the crumbling portico and crossed the tiled floor of the inner courtyard. Her sandalled feet echoed up the old stone steps as she ascended to the top of the fourth terrace. From here she could see near and far and from horizon to horizon in every direction; from the women on their way to the well on the outskirts of the village, or north to the soft white glow of the Himalayas hanging like clouds.

She tucked herself into a segment of shade which slanted sharply from the balustrade and leaned her back against the cool stone. She extricated the envelope from her waist.

R.N.B.

HMS *Terror*

Singapore

3 September 1950

My dear Marvi,

(The words resonated on the page. Patrick's teasing Irish voice came into her head.)

Look where I am. Singapore. Just down the road from you really – give or take a few thousand miles. The navy's great. The places I've seen and the things I've done would fill a book. Of course they work you hard. We're up at five every morning, and then it's drill and kit and spit and polish and practice and training. But the lads are the best, and time off in Singapore is a darn sight better than time off in the Orkneys – I can tell you.

I had a letter from Mammy last week. They're moving out of Whitworth Road at last. They've been given a council house – a brand new one with a separate kitchen and bathroom and three whole bedrooms – can you imagine? It will seem like Buckingham Palace after living in that slum for so long. I hope Kathleen's writing to you. She misses you – God knows why. (Joke.) Michael's doing all right. Still working as a brickie. He's got himself a girl. It's serious. Did Kathy tell you? Her name's Joan Palmer. They're going to

get engaged. Kathy says she's like Jane Wyman. Blimey. I
suppose it'll be wedding bells soon. What about you, Marvi?
I hope they haven't married you off already. Keep in touch.
I'm at the above address for at least two months, so, if you
write straight away, it will get to me.

Well, must stop. Chin chin and TTFN (if you remember
what that means – ta-ta for now).

Love,

Patrick

P.S. Are you still playing the fiddle?

Can you be a ghost while you are still alive? She had heard of
fakirs and holy men with special powers being in two places
at once. Had she not often done the same? Surely they would
see her there in London – in Whitworth Road – climbing the
dark dingy staircase to the first floor. 'Hello, Mr O'Grady!' She
waved at him through the open door where he sat in his usual
chair, with his one remaining leg propped up on the mantel-
piece, swearing and cursing at the world. And there was Mrs
O'Grady doing half a dozen things at once, moving from the
laundry to the cooking to rocking little Beryl or making a
cup of tea or lighting up a cigarette; and Michael stripped to
the waist, washing at the kitchen sink; and Kathleen leaning
out of the window to yell to her friends, who were swinging
round the lamppost; and Patrick – surely Patrick sensed her
ghostly presence following him around as she had never done

in real life, lingering at his shoulder, leaning into his conversations, blushing at his teasing? Did he never feel that she was there?

She pressed his letter to her nose and mouth, and breathed in its smell, then folded it away and stared into nothing. Her elation vanished.

'Have they married you off yet?' he had asked.

'No, not yet,' she said out loud.

'Are you still playing the violin?' he had asked.

'Of course I am. What a silly question.'

The violin was her most precious possession. She had been given it in England by old Dr Silbermann, who had taught her to play. Her father disapproved. He saw it as yet one more thing that made her different, and stopped her from being marriageable. It was true that people in the village had stared and sniggered when she had tried playing at home. Girls round here didn't do that sort of thing. Nobody did that sort of thing – not here. Musicians came along from time to time for weddings and festivals, but when the celebration was over, they moved on. So Marvinder brought her violin to the palace whenever she could, to play it undisturbed.

She went to her secret alcove in the wall where she had stored the violin case, all wrapped in newspaper and swaddled in a cloth bag, to keep away the ants and worms and other creatures which might enjoy feasting on its shining red wood.

She unwrapped it and took it out carefully. Moving to the deepest shade she could find, she began to practise her daily exercises, just as Dr Silbermann had taught her. She drew the full length of the bow up and down the open strings over and over again, until her ear was satisfied and the sound lifted like a bird and soared away into the sky.

She became a ghost again. In London, she had often looked at a single patch of blue sky – whenever there was any blue sky – and imagined it was India. Now here – as a hot blue haze tinged the whole countryside around – she shut her eyes and imagined she was playing to old Dr Silbermann down in his dark, basement flat where the sun hardly got beyond the windowsill.

She read Patrick's letter once more. This time, the words 'stay in touch' gave her hope. 'At least he wants me to stay in touch. I will. I'll write.' She put away her violin with the letter tucked inside.

In one of the empty rooms below, where the dust drifted in the sunbeams – a vast cosmos of golden stars – the watcher sat on his haunches with his back against the wall, waiting like a weather-worn stone statue; featureless but solid. He didn't move when Marvinder descended the stone steps, hurrying. He heard the rustle of her clothes – like angels' wings.

They were king and queen in this ruined palace, moving like chess pieces; silently avoiding each other – for the moment.

2 Secret love

'Aren't you going to school today, Jaspal?'

Nazakhat glanced at his best friend who hacked at a piece of sugar-cane with his knife. The two boys lay side by side in the middle of a dense sugar-cane field – thick enough to hide a tiger. They often helped themselves when the farmer wasn't looking.

'Nah! School's boring. I hate it. Besides, I can read and write already. What's the point of more?'

'Hey man! Your dad will beat you. Remember last time? I thought he'd kill you.'

'I can take it,' shrugged Jaspal.

'Everyone said you were going to be big. Get an important job. Live in the city one of these days. Don't you care? He wanted so much for you.'

'He doesn't know. He thinks I'm there now. Besides, why should I care what my father wants for me – all those diplomas and degrees and bits of paper from his time in England – fat lot of good his learning did for him.'

Nazakhat glanced sideways at him. Jaspal's face had hardened and he became deeply silent. Jaspal was not an easy friend – not like the old days. His mood could change so fast. One minute he could be laughing and joking about like a clown and the next as darkly gloomy as a soldier back from the war.

A final hack severed the cane and Jaspal got to his feet to break it in half across his knee. He gave one half to Nazakhat then flopped down again into the warm earth and chewed on his bit. The fibres burst a flood of sweet sugar into his mouth and he sucked hard. After a while he said, 'Besides, I can't stand sitting with all those goondas – idiots – while this mumbling half-wit tries to teach us useless things which mean nothing. Why, I know more than he does.'

A silence fell between them once more, and Nazakhat could tell that Jaspal would not be the first to break it.

'You know what,' Nazakhat nudged Jaspal in the ribs. 'I think that old devil, Bahadur Singh, has a secret woman somewhere.' He elbowed him in the ribs and shaped a female form in the air with his hands.

'What? Bahadur Singh? You must be crazy!' Jaspal grunted with mild disbelief at the thought of that old fogey, the village schoolmaster, having a secret romance.

'I live under his roof. Wouldn't I know if something was going on?'

Jaspal didn't respond for a while, but sucked on the sugar-cane. At last he said, in a determinedly bored voice, 'Does that mean his aunt knows?'

Nazakhat grinned to himself as he won at least a fraction of Jaspal's attention. 'Oh no! She's deaf and blind to anything like that. She's too busy praying and being holy. She probably doesn't even know where babies come from! Aiee, aiee!' Nazakhat burst out into infectious giggling and even Jaspal couldn't prevent a smile.

'But what makes you think Bahadur Singh has a woman?' asked Jaspal, sceptical but curious.

'I saw him in the bazaar.' Nazakhat leaned forward confidentially. 'He was looking at women's things – you know, cloth pieces, sarees and jewellery.'

'Is that all?' Jaspal's face fell. 'I thought perhaps you'd seen him with someone – you know – ' He gave a wry smile.

Nazakhat, triumphant now at having thoroughly engaged Jaspal's attention, slapped him on the back and rolled about laughing. 'You know, you know!' he mocked raucously.

'Looking at sarees is hardly enough evidence,' shrugged Jaspal.

'Since when would the teacher, a confirmed bachelor, be looking at sarees?' demanded Nazakhat. 'Books – yes. Writing materials – yes. But sarees? I ask you! Wouldn't you wonder who for, if not for a woman?'

'For his aunt?'

'His aunt!' Nazakhat's voice rose with hilarity. 'She's no woman!' He was really enjoying himself now as Jaspal began to snigger too, despite himself. 'She never wears sarees – only salwaar kameez – and only ever grey.'

'Blue,' corrected Jaspal.

'Call that blue?' cried Nazakhat. 'It's not the blue of the sky. It's not the blue of peacock feathers or of kingfishers or even of your turban. Anyway, I should know. My father made that outfit for her before . . .' before he was killed along with the rest of my family '. . . and he called it grey. He used to make all her outfits – and they were all grey or some colour so dull it might as well be grey. Anyway, Bahadur Singh was looking at really glittery sarees and cloth pieces: red and pink, and silks with embroidered borders and lots of gold and silver threads, so it wasn't for his aunt – you can be sure of that.'

'Perhaps she's make believe.' Jaspal began to forget his troubles. He sat up, fantasising. 'You know – wishful thinking. He feels deprived. He wants to love. He has invented a beautiful woman all bumps and curves like that film star, Devaki Rani. He can't have her for real – but he pretends – what do you think, eh, Nazakhat? He whispers her name into his pillow at night. "Oh, Devaki, Devaki! I can't live without you . . ." '

The boys rolled about shrieking with laughter as their jokes got more and more vivid. 'Don't you think I have a good theory?' cried Jaspal. 'Perhaps Bahadur Singh has a whole secret store of sarees and jewellery. He realises that he's spent too much time with his books and that crabby old aunt. That the world and all its women are passing him by and he hasn't yet lived!'

'I'm serious, bhai!' insisted Nazakhat, when their laughter died down. 'He has been looking in jewellery shops — no kidding. I've seen him. I'm not making this up. There is someone, I know it.'

'Well then, it is his aunt,' said Jaspal with mock seriousness. 'He loves her thin scraggy arms and her hatchet face and her beautiful body as shapely as an ancient camel. Or . . . or . . . !' Jaspal got to his knees and looked deeply serious. 'His aunt has been made an offer she can't refuse and Bahadur Singh is providing her dowry!' The boys' hilarity rang out through the sugar-cane.

'Shut up, shut up! The farmer will hear us!' hissed Jaspal, and they clamped their syrupy mouths.

'But I ask you, bhai, who would he give jewellery to?' Nazakhat whispered through his fingers. 'Have you ever seen his aunt wearing anything but the silver kara on her wrist and two gold studs in her ears?'

'You have a point,' Jaspal conceded. 'But you live there. You see everything. Come on, think. If there is someone, you must know.'

'Perhaps he got her from a newspaper ad,' reflected Nazakhat. 'I'll find out one of these days.'

'You're wrong. You must be. He wouldn't marry.' Jaspal finally hacked off another piece of cane and started to strip away the outside. 'He's not the marrying kind. Here.' Jaspal handed Nazakhat the white fibrous stalk, dripping with sugar, and proceeded to hack one for himself.

A distant shriek of the train whistle made them sit up.

'It's the Amritsar train.' Jaspal leaped to his feet, his gloom fully vanished and his eyes now sparkling with enterprise. 'Let's catch it – eh, bhai?'

'Are you going to school after all?' Jaspal's school was the intermediate college in Amritsar.

'Nah! I feel like going to the pictures. Will you come?'

Nazakhat got to his feet. He was nervous about going into town. He loved films too, but, as a Muslim, he was afraid of going out of his neighbourhood. Memories of the past were still fresh. But Jaspal grabbed his arm warmly. 'Come on, bhai. Say yes.'

'Your school though, what about school?' Nazakhat asked weakly.

'Oh, to hell with school! Come on!'

This was good old Jaspal. Nazakhat couldn't resist. 'Get a move on then,' he yelled, pushing ahead.

They chucked away the sugar-cane and thrashed their way out of the field. They heard the whistle again. Nearer this time. They were running full pelt. They reached the edge of the long white road, dashed over and plunged down the dyke disappearing into the waves of barley. They re-emerged on the path dividing the saffron crop from the mustard seed.

'Hey, wait for me, Jaspal!' yelled Nazakhat. He clutched his side as a stitch seared through his guts. Jaspal only slowed down sufficiently to glance over his shoulder and to give an encouraging yell. 'Get on with it! We'll miss it!'

A long streak of grey smoke in the sky straggled out like the hair of an old woman who shakes away the tangles of sleep. And again the siren; closer now, its pitch screaming out intervals as the train slowed down. Good old Hari Singh, the engine driver. He has relatives in this village. He does them a favour by slowing down here.

From out of nowhere, figures came leaping up the embankment along the track and others, like the boys, raced along the paths through the fields, as the great black, iron goddess approached with burning fiery belly and smoke belching out of her ears. She was many-headed and many-armed, flailing with limbs from the bodies which hung from her carriages and clung to the roof.

'Make room, make room!' shouted voices panting with exertion. They sprinted alongside with arms outstretched. It was each one for himself now. Jaspal noted a space the size of a hand on the vertical steel pole by one of the doors. He focused on it, running faster and faster. It was now or never as gradually the train began to pick up steam once more. He grabbed with one hand. It tugged his feet from beneath him, and only the friendly hands of others saved him from being dragged along, or dashed back on to the sharp chippings of the track.

He managed to find enough toe room on the wooden running board, and with both hands, he gripped the pole. His body arched from the train like a bow, the wind billowing his shirt. And so he stayed, hanging on for dear life, until Amritsar. But he laughed – an open-mouthed laugh, eating the air – and felt a pure, fierce joy.

He looked up and down the length of the train. Did Nazakhat make it?

He couldn't see him beside the track, so he must have got on somewhere. They would meet up later.

'Hey Jaspal! Are you going to the pictures?' someone bellowed.

'Yeah! It's a Prithviraj Kapoor film today!' Jaspal yelled back.

'See you at the Rialto then.'

Jaspal loved going to the pictures. Often, he went alone, on afternoons when he should have been at school. He didn't mind seeing the same film over and over again – even if each time it meant sneaking in without paying – especially the historical films about battles between rajahs and invading armies, and brave warriors of the past.

The outskirts of the city undulated into sight: walls and roofs and balconies hanging with washing; narrow alleys and streets teeming with people and animals. Black, long-haired pigs foraged in the rubbish tips, ambling alongside dogs and crows and other scavengers. Monkeys lined the walls, preening each other, slapping their little ones into line as they tumbled and played.

The train slowed down to give the tens of dozens of non-ticket holders a chance to drop from the train before it entered the station precincts. Jaspal lowered himself till his feet were running along the ground, then he loosened his grip and continued running to gain his balance.

Nazakhat caught up with him and the two left the track and headed across rough ground towards the city. Nazakhat always felt a little nervous about coming into the city. Although he had allowed his wispy boy's moustache to grow, and his hair was thick and black and long to his shoulders, he was conspicuously not a Sikh like Jaspal. The vicious troubles of partition were still too fresh in people's memories to enable him to feel comfortable. He would never have ventured there without Jaspal at his side.

The new Pakistan had wanted Amritsar too. 'But what about our Golden Temple?' protested the enraged Sikhs. 'Only over our dead bodies will our Golden Temple go into Pakistan with the Muslims.' And there were many dead bodies before it was certain that Amritsar would stay part of India.

Nazakhat knew that any trips into the city meant he had to brave the taunts from gangs jeering, 'What is that blood-drained, meat-eating, son of a pig-dog, hair-cutting Muslim doing, contaminating our holy city?' But Jaspal had always been Nazakhat's stout and loyal defender, and had got into many a brawl protecting him from mobs of youths out for trouble.

There were a few hours to kill before joining the queue which would start forming outside the Rialto. The boys headed into the bazaar. They liked to go to the metal area where they sold not only pots and pans, farming tools and kitchen utensils, but knives and daggers and swords of all descriptions. They fingered the sharp blades and counted their money. They knew they didn't have enough, so after a lot of comparing and exchanging knowledge and expertise about the lethal nature of this weapon or that, and what kind of wound it could inflict, the shopkeeper realised they weren't going to buy, and shooed them away. So they went to a tea stall and bought tea and samosas, and sat at a bare wooden table and grinned at each other and gripped each other's hands – elbows on the table – to see who could force the other's hand down first and prove the stronger.

'Hey! Speak of the devil! Quick!' Nazakhat grabbed Jaspal and thrust his head down under the table. 'It's Bahadur Singh, I tell you. I just saw him! Boy, would I be in trouble if he caught me here.'

'Take it easy. What are you so scared of?' drawled Jaspal. 'He never lays a finger on you.'

'Yeah – but you should feel the hand of his aunt round your ear. She's worse than any man. She hits so hard, all her bones rattle.'

'Well, my father hits so hard you can't hear anything for the blood pounding inside your head and the screams in your lungs you're trying to stifle. But what do I care? I can take it,' boasted Jaspal.

The two boys peered out of the tea stall.

'There! Look! There. He's heading into the cloth quarter. Hey! What do you think?' Nazakhat clutched his friend's arm. 'Maybe he's got a secret assignment with his lady friend.'

'Come on, let's follow him.' Jaspal's curiosity was up. 'I've got to see this.'

'For god's sake be careful. It's all right for you. You don't care about anything. But me – if he sees me – he could throw me out.' Nazakhat hung back warily.

'So what! Look how you survived before. You don't need him. Don't be such a chicken. Anyway – you can see he's got things on his mind. He won't notice us. Come on, before we lose him.' Jaspal dragged his friend out into the road.

A cluster of young women, chaperoned by a much older one, jostled their way down the narrow bazaar street in front of the schoolmaster. They stopped every two or three steps to peer into the sandal shop, or the cosmetic shop, or the woollens shop. Bahadur Singh could have pushed through them any time, but seemed instead to want to follow just on

24

the edges, as if he were looking at what they looked at and listening to all their comments.

The boys followed more boldly. They watched the schoolmaster watching. They watched too – suddenly seeing the women's world with men's eyes – smelling their scent and hearing the tinkle of bangles as arms lifted to hold up glittering materials, which hung from hooks outside the shop; or bales of cloth arranged in towers from ceiling to floor, ready at a mere whim to be extricated and tossed full length across the carpeted shop floor. High voices and laughter rose above the hubbub of the bazaar.

Bahadur Singh turned abruptly. The boys ducked. When they next peered out, the schoolmaster had given up on the women and moved on to the jewellery quarter.

'See? Didn't I tell you? It's what I saw him doing in our bazaar. This must be serious, I tell you. Why else would he come to Amritsar? He's got money to spend.'

They spied on the schoolmaster moving from one jewellery shop to another, glancing at the displays, listening sometimes to the shopkeepers' patter over an offered cup of tea, then moving on. The boys hardly bothered to hide now. The schoolmaster was too absorbed, poring over the trays of bangles and earrings and necklaces.

'Watch out!' Jaspal pulled Nazakhat down behind a wandering cow. The schoolmaster had stopped in front of a jeweller's shop. He paused a long time to gaze at something, then suddenly looked round as if checking whether anyone was watching him.

'That was a near thing!' breathed Jaspal.

'Did he see us?'

'Nah! He wouldn't have gone in if he had. You're right, Nazakhat. He's up to something, the old devil! Let's get a little nearer.'

The two boys sidled up to the shop and flopped on the wooden steps in front, next to a dog and a resting holy man. A useful alleyway ran alongside, down which they could disappear when Bahadur Singh came out.

It was dark inside the shop. On a wooden counter gleamed a pair of brass scales. Bahadur Singh sat on the stool, his back to the door, facing the old jeweller, who scrutinised him from over his gold-rimmed spectacles.

'Can I help you?' the jeweller asked.

'I am looking for a simple gift for my daughter,' they heard the schoolmaster reply.

'Didn't you hear that? Daughter, my foot!' exclaimed Jaspal.

'Didn't I tell you! Didn't I tell you!' chortled Nazakhat triumphantly.

'Shut up, you idiot! You'll give us away. Look. Now what's he doing?'

'Ah!' The jeweller's exclamation was dry but business-like, as if he already knew exactly what was suitable for the schoolmaster. He bent down, and from beneath the counter brought out three glass cases filled with rings, gold and silver chains, earrings, nose studs, necklaces and bracelets – of an infinite variety of precious stone. His eyes hovered over Bahadur's hands as they fingered the different items of jewellery in a tentative and inexperienced way. He noted that they were not the hands of a farmer or an artisan because they were too smooth, so he deduced that his client was a clerk or a teacher who wouldn't want anything gaudy or too ostentatious.

The jeweller selected a simple gold bracelet. 'Is this to your liking?' he asked.

Bahadur held the bracelet in the palm of his hand. Jaspal stared at it too. Its cold metal burned in the dark, dusty air like the outer rim of the sun. Whose wrist did the schoolmaster see it encircling?

'Yes, this is to my liking,' said Bahadur Singh, getting out a wodge of rupee notes from an inside pocket.

'What's he buying?' whispered Nazakhat.

'A bracelet,' murmured Jaspal. 'A gold bracelet. I wonder who it's for?'

3 The dividing sword

The queue was already long when Jaspal and Nazakhat reached the Rialto. It was always long and it always looked as though they would never get in. But experience had taught them that they would, even if it meant squeezing through a forest of legs to get to the front.

They burst through the curtain into the warm, pungent darkness, threw themselves into the springy seats, which squeaked if they wriggled, and with heads tipped back, stared at the big screen in front of them. Soon images and loud music overwhelmed them and sucked them out of reality into the wonderful fantasy worlds of heroes and princesses, dancing girls and warriors and treacherous enemies.

As soon as Nazakhat saw what this film was about, he wished he hadn't come. 'Arreh, brother. I thought we were seeing a Hindi film. What's this?'

Jaspal shrugged, 'Oh, a new one in Punjabi,' he muttered. 'I thought it might be worth seeing.' The changing light of the screen flickered over his face and he looked like one in a trance.

The film was about the great eighteenth century hero of Sikhism, Baba Deep Singh, the leader who had defended the Golden Temple of Amritsar against invading Afghan Muslims with only a gathering of peasants bearing nothing but staves. Even after his head had been cut off, the stories related with relish how Baba Deep Singh, carrying his head in one hand and a sword in the other, had continued to fight to protect the Golden Temple from desecration by the Muslims.

Jaspal had seen many pictures depicting this event and heard many stories at the gurudwara, but never before had it come alive for him. Never before had he felt so moved and inspired as he did watching this film. He became a part of the history and the struggle. It was happening now and, overcome with passion, his thoughts spun with anger. If only he could be such a warrior. What cause was there now worth fighting for? As if reading his thoughts, Baba Deep Singh's face filled the screen. He turned, as if searching into the soul of every single person in the dark cinema.

Was it possible . . . ? For a moment, Jaspal's credibility was suspended. He shrank away, terrified by the warrior's penetrating gaze. He buried his face in his hands and fearfully peered through his fingers at the powerful head towering above them. Jaspal felt sucked into the dark pools of his eyes which stared at him and him alone; challenging him, questioning him. They seemed to say, what are you doing with your life – wasting it away as if you will live for ever? Free yourself from the bonds of desire and act, for action is greater than inaction. Then Baba Deep Singh whirled his sword against his enemies.

The whole cinema was on its feet, Jaspal too, cheering him on – howling at these Afghan enemies who dared to defile the sacred temple.

Nazakhat sank lower and lower in his seat. He dreaded the moment when the lights would come up and everyone would recognise him as the Muslim enemy. Before the film ended, he whispered to Jaspal, 'I'm dying for a pee. I'll meet you outside.' He wriggled himself out of the row and escaped from the seething darkness of the cinema.

For the next twenty minutes, Nazakhat hung about outside waiting for the film to end. At last the doors were flung open and the thick velvet curtains tossed aside. Usually, when the boys came jostling out, they were still part of the film. They carried on the action, chasing and play-fighting and quoting back all their favourite bits. But today was different. The men, nearly all of them Sikhs, some of them Hindus, but no Muslims, poured from the cinema, their eyes shining with excited fervour. Nazakhat, sheltering behind one of the pillars in the foyer, strained to find Jaspal. Then he saw him. Jaspal looked dazed, walking slowly, while everyone around him swirled past.

'There you are!' exclaimed Nazakhat, leaping out and linking arms.

Jaspal turned and looked at him blankly, as if he were a stranger. He withdrew his arm and moved away – almost imperceptibly – but Nazakhat knew.

They came out into the street.

'Hey!' cried Nazakhat playfully. 'What's up with you?' and he jumped on his friend's back and tried to tussle him into a play fight.

'Get off!' growled Jaspal.

At first Nazakhat carried on, teasing and goading, trying to provoke him into action. Jaspal threw him off so roughly that he tumbled to the ground.

'Yeah!' laughed Nazakhat, thinking it was all in fun. Then he saw Jaspal's face. It was frozen in anger. His eyes were narrowed and his lips tight. 'Hey, Jaspal! You OK?'

'Just leave off will you!' Jaspal muttered vehemently and walked ahead through the bazaar.

Nazakhat got to his feet, amazed and disturbed. Jaspal could be moody, he knew that, but this was the first time he had felt his hostility; an enmity even.

Instead of heading for the railway station, Jaspal turned towards the old quarter of the city.

'Eh, bhai! Brother!' Nazakhat called uneasily. 'Aren't you going home? The train goes in ten minutes. We haven't got too much time.'

'You go,' shouted Jaspal over his shoulder. 'There's something I want to do,' and he strode away even faster, disappearing into the throng of the bazaar.

Nazakhat stood, unable to move for a minute or two. First and foremost he longed to catch up with his friend and beg his forgiveness for whatever it was he had done to make him angry. Surely he didn't blame him for the actions of those Afghan Muslims in the film? But the thought of his cold, unfriendly face restrained him. With an uncomprehending shrug he carried on to the station.

Doubts overwhelmed Nazakhat. Were not he and Jaspal still the best of friends? He looked at the scar on the palm of his hand. They were blood brothers. Their history went back a long way. They both remembered – had nightmares of remembering – when their village was burned and all around them people – their own friends and neighbours and families – were massacred. Yet, how, despite the danger, first Jaspal's family had sheltered Nazakhat's family when a band of Sikhs came burning and driving out all Muslims; and then how Nazakhat's family had protected Jaspal and his mother and sister when Muslims came on a murderous raid, intent on revenge, killing any Sikh they could find and burning down all their property.

Everyone had gone mad with blood lust, but the two families, Nazakhat's and Jaspal's, had never betrayed each other, and their friendship stayed true till the end, when Jhoti and her children finally fled.

It was two years before Jaspal returned to his village. The two friends had greeted each other joyfully – hardly able to believe that the other was alive. Bit by bit, Jaspal learned the terrible fate which had befallen Nazakhat's family.

'They came again,' whispered Nazakhat.

Both knew 'they' meant the jathas, the Sikh war bands who had ruthlessly tried to defend what they saw as their homeland. It was because of the splitting of the Punjab into two. One part in India would be ruled by Hindus and the other part in Pakistan would be ruled by Muslims. The Sikhs could not accept it, and fought like trapped tigers. Should they not have a homeland too?

'We should have got out earlier,' said Nazakhat despairingly. 'Gone to the Pakistan part – but this has been our home for generations. We all lived like brothers – Sikhs, Muslims and Hindus. We thought we could see it through. But the jathas were like crazed demons,' he wept. 'I saw them all killed – my father and brothers – with swords and knives. They showed no mercy; not even for my mother, my sisters or my grandmother.'

'How did you escape?' Jaspal had whispered, hardly able to comprehend such a loss.

'I don't know. I just don't know. I was there. I saw my little brother dying. I held him in my arms. I nursed him and rocked him and begged him not to die. A Sikh saw me. He raised his sword and brought it down to strike off my head. I felt its wind as it slashed past my ear, but it just crashed into the ground beside me and he didn't touch me. After that, it was as though I was invisible. They went on slaughtering – any Muslim they could find – and burning and screaming. I just sat there with my dead brother in the middle of it all – the smoke, the flames and the blood – until they went. Then there was a silence – a terrible silence. More terrible than anything. No one moaned or stirred or called out even to God. No dog howled. No vulture screeched. No wind blew. It was a hell of non-existence. Why didn't they kill me, Jaspal? Why?'

'Because,' Jaspal said as softly as a stalking tiger, 'because they recognised you as a brother. My brother. Look.' Jaspal took out his kirpan – his dagger. He held out his left hand and slashed its palm. Red drops of blood immediately spouted. 'Will you be my blood brother?' he asked, staring intently at Nazakhat. Without a word, Nazakhat held out his left hand and allowed Jaspal to slash it. As the blood flowed, the two boys clasped hands and rubbed their palms together and then licked the mingled blood.

'Brothers for ever!' cried Jaspal.

'Brothers for ever!' Nazakhat agreed joyfully.

Nazakhat stared now at the faint scar which crossed the fate line and life line of his palm. He felt a great chasm of despair opening up inside his stomach. 'Brothers for ever?'

4 The sparrow meets the hawk

When Jaspal left Nazakhat after the film, he headed for the Golden Temple. That was where the action in the film had taken place. Jaspal had been to the temple many times. Now, all he wanted was to step on that dazzling white marble and imagine Baba Deep Singh whirling his sword in defence of the temple. He wanted to see where the blood had been spilled and hear the clash of swords and spears.

He wound his way through the bazaar, looking neither to the right nor the left; ignoring the teeming shops and hawkers yelling their wares, until at last he was outside the great white façade.

He removed his sandals, washed his hands and feet, and joined a flurry of families entering the complex. The fathers and sons strode ahead, their turbaned heads held high; while the mothers and sisters, lost among their billowing cotton trousers and veiled heads, herded the little ones along.

He reached the top of steep marble steps. Below him, the vast pool of holy water, the amrit, the nectar of ecstasy, glittered too bright to bear.

Suddenly, he was alone, even though hundreds milled around him. He descended the steps and on to the intricate inlaid patterns of the marble terrace. At first, he just walked, so unaware of his feet on the cool marble that he might as well have been floating. He walked between the colonnade of pillars, his eye fixed on the golden shrine which jutted out into the centre of the lake, as if the craftsmen of the temple had tried to recreate the sun.

On and on he walked, seeing not the peaceful families and pilgrims who moved in a quiet throng but the shrieks and screams of fighting warriors, their blood spewing across the white marble, and the lake strewn with bodies and limbs. Jaspal thought of martyrs and saints and wondered what qualities were needed to be a martyr. Could he survive pain and torture and look death in the face? He had felt hatred many times, but now his hatred was mixed with a new sensation; that of ecstasy.

He stopped and undressed down to his shorts. He unwound his turban and bared his head with his hair bound into a topknot. Hiding his knife among his clothes, he descended the steps into the pool and lowered himself into the water. It was silk-cool. Down, down he went, till the water was up to his chest – and then – immersed himself completely.

In the refracting light he seemed to see, not the tumbling bodies of dying Muslim enemies and Sikh warriors, but other images, which try as he might, would not go away; images of those English children, their golden heads with streaming hair and wide blue, puzzled eyes, which couldn't believe that only water poured in through their open mouths.

And why not me, Lord? Why not me? Jaspal cried in his head. Why had he not drowned too along with Ralph and Grace when the boat went down in the palace lake? They were his friends. He couldn't deny it. He had loved them too – even though they were English. Jaspal tried to forget the events which happened six years ago, when together they had crossed over the threshold into the realms of death. Whatever other terrible sights he had witnessed, nothing else had brought him closer to death, and he couldn't prevent the unbidden image; the unexpected voice or sound; the glint of sun on water. It would trigger the memory, and that long sad afternoon would unwind, forcing him to live those moments again and again. He remembered the pale bodies sinking down, their arms and legs waving like strange plants. Then, just as he and the twins were about to let loose their souls for ever, Marvinder brought him back to the living and the twins were left behind in the land of death. Today it struck him. Perhaps there was a reason why he and only he had lived. Perhaps he had been saved for a purpose.

His air gave out. He thrust himself to the surface gasping and choking.

'Ha!' A voice called from the side. 'You were under a long time. I was just about to jump in and pull you out.'

Knuckling the water from his eyes, Jaspal looked to see who addressed him. Night had fallen. The golden dome of the temple glowed like an eclipsed sun behind the figure, and silhouetted a man as he knelt at the side of the tank. Bending into the darkness, it seemed to Jaspal that a giant waited at the side watching him – a giant of a warrior with a high pleated turban and a great curving sword glistening at his belt.

Jaspal waded up the steps and stood dripping and un-certain. He squeezed the water out of his hair and clothes.

'Here, have this,' said the man as if it were an order, and handed him a thin towel. He was on his feet now and towered above the boy.

Obediently, Jaspal began to dry himself. Bending to towel his arms and legs, he stole glances at the guardian warrior. The flickering oil lamps brought colour and focus. The man's height wasn't an illusion. He was very tall. Well over six foot, but gaunt and thin like a ravaged tree. His high dark blue turban made him seem even taller and more imposing. But it was not just his height which was impressive, it was his thick, black, long beard; his mouth, with strangely chewed lips which, when he smiled, revealed uneven teeth with gaps, but white as pearl. His nose, which had once been broken, jutted out like the beak of a hunting bird. His cheeks hollowed into the prominent bone structure of his skull. His brow was like the overhang of a cliff, under which his eyes seemed to hide, disappearing into narrow crevices, but suddenly reappearing, wide, black and mesmerising, as if they could see and control your very soul.

As Jaspal began to shake out his topknot to dry his hair, the warrior strolled away. Jaspal watched him patrol all the way round the pool, casual as a tiger. By the time he returned, Jaspal was combing out his hair with great care, catching the strands in the teeth of the comb and allowing the warm night air to dry them.

'The priest is reading from the Guru Granth Sahib now,' said the man. 'You will go and listen.'

Jaspal wasn't sure if it was a question or a command, but he nodded and quickly knotted up his hair and rewound his turban round his head. He followed the guardian warrior towards the Golden Temple. It was like walking into the very heart of the sun. He wasn't sure if he was being accompanied or escorted by the giant, who was both behind him and before him, for the warrior's long, black shadow enveloped him as he walked along the causeway. He entered the brightly lit hall and sat cross-legged on a carpet before a raised platform on which a priest sat before a huge book, the Guru Granth Sahib.

The priest's voice droned on and on. To his side, an attendant fanned him rhythmically. Jaspal felt like a vessel which had been emptied, but was now being filled again with something new – something that his body and soul needed for survival.

When the reading finished, the warrior beckoned Jaspal to follow. They left the main hall and went back along the causeway to the colonnade and into one of the prayer rooms off to one side. The warrior took out an old book and began flicking through the pages. 'What brings you here so often?' he asked, his eyes still on the pages which he turned. 'I've noticed you. You come often, but always alone. Have you no family?'

'Yes, sir,' said Jaspal. 'But they are out in the village. I come in on the train.'

'Why do you come here to the temple? Has some voice spoken to you in the stillness of your heart about God and his prophets?'

Jaspal looked up – his face so coldly blank that even the warrior flinched under the chill gaze. 'No voice, sir!' Jaspal answered. 'Just a feeling . . . ?'

'A feeling?' the warrior repeated.

'A sort of feeling – that there is something that has to be done. Something I have to do. I don't yet know . . .' his voice trailed away, embarrassed.

'Can you read?'

'Yes, sir.'

'Read this.' The priest opened a holy book.

Jaspal ran his finger along the Punjabi script.

> 'There is one God:
> His name is Truth;
> The All-Pervading Creator.'

He read slowly but fluently, being more familiar with English script than Punjabi.

'Do you go to school?'

Jaspal shrugged. 'I'm supposed to but . . .'

'But?' The voice was severe.

'It's boring. I know it all. I need more.

'What does your father do?'

'He was a scholar and a soldier, but – he's a farmer now. He works his inheritance.'

'Will you be a farmer too?'

'I thought I would, when I was in England, but now . . .' He paused.

'Now?' The priest's voice was low and searching.

Jaspal shrugged. 'I don't know.'

The priest shut the book and closed his eyes deep in thought. 'We need hawks. You are nothing but a sparrow.'

The guardian warrior led him out of the sanctum. 'Have you thought of being a priest?'

Jaspal stared. No. No. Inside him the word was no.

'Think about it. But what our revered master meant was that we need our priests to be hawks. Think about the qualities of a hawk, and if you think you have them, come back to me. Come here and ask for Amarjit Singh.'

Nazakhat must have slept. Curled up in one of the railway arches alongside the track. It was dark when he awoke. He had deliberately missed the last train, unwilling to abandon Jaspal in the town. It was not the first time they had had to walk back in the darkness, following the gleaming serpentine rails. He shook himself with annoyance. He hadn't intended to sleep. Now he must have missed Jaspal.

He got to his feet and stared down the track. In the far distance he could see the spotlight of an approaching train, powerful as Lord Shiva's third eye, destroying any darkness which came within its gaze. It caught a figure standing at the side of the track. Nazakhat knew it was Jaspal before the cone of dazzling white light moved on, leaving him plunged in a black void.

The train passed hissing and spitting; grinding steel upon

steel. Golden sparks splattered the night. The sound was thunderous and deafening. A brief and awesome orange hole slid by within which half-naked, black figures shovelled coal as if stoking up the fires of hell. Then oblivion.

Nazakhat waited a long time for the sound of the train to die away before shouting, 'Brother!' He began to walk along the rails unable to see if Jaspal had heard him and was bothering to wait.

There was no answer. He walked for an hour, alone in the darkness, with only a vague glint of new moon on the rails. It would be at least another hour of walking before he reached Deri. He began to sing a film song to cheer himself up, striding across the sleepers between the rails. Then he became aware that he was not alone. Pacing him on the path alongside was a figure. Nazakhat knew it was Jaspal.

He stopped singing. 'So you're there.'

No answer.

'Why are you angry?'

No answer.

'Did I do something to offend you, brother?'

No answer.

'Where did you go?'

No answer.

Nazakhat felt a pang of unease. 'Why do you not speak?' he asked.

'Speaking is useless,' said Jaspal in a low, distinct voice.

'How else can one communicate?' asked Nazakhat.

'There are other ways.'

'Such as?' Nazakhat waited for Jaspal to say more but he didn't, so Nazakhat began singing again at the top of his voice, so as not to walk the rest of the way to the village in silence.

5 The whispering stones

The heat hangs over the land like an open mouth, its swollen tongue too parched even to lick its lips. The farmer's hoe has dropped from his hand. He lies beneath a tree, still as a corpse, his breathing too shallow to raise his chest.

It is at this time that the watcher feels most powerful. He climbs to the highest terrace of the palace, and with the burning sun poised directly over his head, throws off his shawl and reveals his horrible, featureless face. He is in the realm of the living but feels like an emissary from the dead. He surveys the land all around. He claims it for his own, as far as the eye can see.

He claims the people too; just by seeing them he feels he controls them – even those who, like him, will stay awake through the heat of the day; like Jhoti. He watches her gliding down the long white road to the graveyard of All Saints Church, keeping her promise of years ago, to tend an English grave. On the way, she will snap off a sprig of sprawling bougainvillaea and pluck scarlet blossoms from the tulip tree to take to the marble-faced tomb. After she has cleared away a few tangled thorns and wiped the dust from the inlaid inscriptions, which identify the incumbents as *Ralph and Grace Chadwick aged 6 years, Gone to be with Jesus*, she will stretch herself out among the shadows of the memorial crosses and statues and die for a while.

The watcher sees all this with the bored indifference of an all-powerful ruler. He sees without looking because he is waiting for someone else.

Dear Patrick,

Thank you very much for your letter.

Singapore sounds very interesting.

I am so glad you are enjoying the navy.

I wish I could go on a boat again, but I don't expect I ever will.

I am so happy to hear that Ma and Kathleen and every-one have moved into a house. I hope Kathleen will write to me soon and tell me all about it. I expect Kathleen will be a bridesmaid if Michael is getting married. Lucky thing. Will Ma make her a beautiful dress? I wish I could be a bridesmaid with her. Joan Palmer sounds very nice. No wonder Michael loves her if she looks like Doris Day. Will you be able to go to the wedding?

No, I'm not married yet, though my father thinks I should be. He keeps looking out for someone. He even put an ad in the city newspaper, but no one has asked for me. It's because I went to England alone, with only Jaspal, so now they think badly of me. I'm glad. Remember how you said you couldn't marry someone you didn't love? But if someone asks for me and my father says I must, then I won't have a choice. I hope people go on thinking I'm bad, then no one will ask for me.

Yes, I'm still playing the violin, though my father doesn't like me to. He thinks it turns people away too.

If your ship stops in India, I hope you will come and visit us. Jaspal would love to see you too. He remembers going to the baths on your motorbike. He would love to have a motorbike more than anything. He is attending school here, but hates it. He always hated school in England too. He's a very wild boy and I worry about him. Perhaps he should go into the navy.

Please come and see us if you can.

Much love from,

Marvi

She had brought her writing materials to the palace, – a dip pen, a pot of ink and a writing pad. She kneeled on the flag-stoned floor of the upper terrace, crouching over the paper, thinking out her sentences and trying not to smudge. She chewed the end of her metal-nibbed pen, then dipped it into the ink pot.

Marvinder finished writing. She placed four small stones on each corner of the page, then decided to play her violin while the ink was drying. She pulled the violin out of its hiding-place and climbed the last small set of steps which took her to the very highest point of the building. She drew the bow across the strings. The sound vibrated all the way deep inside her. It was a good sound – and she wished old Dr Silbermann could hear it.

After a while, she came back down. The ink would be dry. She was about to remove the stones she had used to hold down the page and take up her letter, when something caught her eye. She stopped, puzzled. She remembered the stones. They had been different shades of grey and white and one was red. She was sure she had put the red stone in the bottom left-hand corner, but now it was up at the top.

A shadow moved across the wall as silent as a cloud.

Marvinder hung over the page like a bird caught in a current of air, her thoughts hovering. The eyes without lashes or the protection of eyebrows and lids watched her.

Marvinder drew back from her letter. She leaned her body

hard against the wall and closed her eyes. Perhaps she slept or half slept. The stones seemed to breathe. Strange reverberations shivered through her back like whispers. She fancied that she heard odd words which didn't come from her brain or out of her mouth, but were whispered through the thick walls. It was as though her own thoughts were translating themselves into sound. They rose and fell out of a babble of murmuring voices like a crowd of people speaking in many different tongues – all foreign to her – except that every now and then a word would rise, make sense, then fall again.

'I want . . .'

She turned and pressed her mouth to the stones. 'Did you say, I want?' she sighed. 'I don't know what I want.'

Time drifted. The ink dried. At last she roused herself. She took away the four stones from the letter and arranged them in a row. From left to right she placed them in order of shade from darkest grey to white. The red one she placed last, just a little apart from the rest. She re-read her letter to Patrick. She put the letter into the violin case. Gathering up her violin and cloth bag with her writing materials, she left the palace roof, gliding down and down the steps, terrace by terrace, till she reached the courtyard at the bottom. Before she went out through the main gateway, she glanced up. A sapling swayed as if held aside. She stared at it without knowing why. A squirrel suddenly spiralled to the ground.

The next time she returned to the palace and examined

the stones they had been re-arranged, left to right from white to darkest grey. The red one was still placed last.

6 The drum beats again

Just round the lake from the palace is a tomb. It is quite a large tomb, raised high on a thick stone dais and encompassed by a spacious stone dome. Once, the surface of the dome would have been faced with brilliant turquoise tiles and inlaid with precious stone: agate, jet, beryl, onyx and amber, for the tomb contained the body of an important Muslim saint. Beautiful flowing designs of flowers and leaves would have entwined with the Arabic letters of the Koran to decorate the arched doorway. White marble steps would have led from the marble terrace down, deep down, into the marble tomb of the revered saint, strewn with marigolds, and glowing in the flickering light of one single oil lamp.

That was five hundred years before, when the Moguls

ruled with absolute power and built their tombs and palaces all over the land. But even when battle after battle finally weakened their might, and holy sites were pillaged and stripped of their treasures, a guardian had always kept watch at the tomb. Every night, until partition, people fell asleep to the heartbeat of a single drum and the chanting from the Koran and, no matter what their creed, felt reassured and protected from evil spirits.

Then, one day, the drum beat ceased. An eerie silence fell over the community. No one could remember a time when the drum hadn't been beating. Suddenly, they realised what they had done to each other. They had turned neighbours into enemies; they had murdered each other and, in the slaughter, they had destroyed something of themselves. The heart stopped. The last guardian was slain and there was no one to take his place. Defaced and bare down to the dark-brown stone, the tomb sank into the undergrowth and was not forgotten, but people were too ashamed to remember.

Just when everyone was getting used to the silence, the drum beat was heard again all round the district, even as far away as the schoolmaster's house.

In the dead of night, Nazakhat awoke, at first unsure why he had woken. Was it the full moon? The room seemed to float in an ocean of brightness. He felt the cosmic tug of the tides, even though he was a thousand miles from any shore. A dog was barking furiously. But it was not the dog, nor the full moon which had woken him. It was the sound of drumming.

He lay there, listening, trying to remember how long it had been since a drum had beaten at the tomb. It was certainly before. Before. Before. Before everything changed. But who would go to the old deserted Muslim tomb? Who was left to go? Who would dare?

He glanced across to the other bed where Jungli slept. It was Nazakhat's job to guard this strange wild child who the village schoolmaster had taken in under his roof. But the creature was still more savage animal than human child; he still preferred the night to the day; sleeping in trees rather than a bed; and running on all fours instead of upright on two. On the whole, he had stopped snarling, biting, scratching and ripping other people's arms, hands, faces, clothes and belongings, but he was wily, cunning, secretive, nimble and with the ability to disappear into nowhere, as if he had magic powers.

The bed was empty. The sheet was a twisted vortex as though Jungli had been sucked away through the bed. Nazakhat pulled the sheet off and shook it out. He had sometimes found the boy tightly knotted right into the very centre. This time, nothing. Jungli had gone. Nazakhat stood staring at the empty bed. Undecided, bewildered by the drumming, he wriggled into shirt and shorts and stepped out on to the verandah. It could almost be dawn, the moonlight was so bright. The drumming was louder; insistent; Nazakhat put his hands to his face and knelt towards Mecca. 'Salaam, allah, *salaam,*' he sang softly, as once the mullah would have sung from the top of the minaret. '*Allahu-Akbar, Ash-ahdu-an-la-ilaha-illalah.*'

Who had come back? He was afraid, yet unable to keep away. He began to walk towards the deserted tomb. The odd figure or two had emerged into the lane, confused by the sound of the mysterious drummer. They gathered in nervous clusters, wondering who had come back to this tomb. Had anyone noticed anything?

Nazakhat avoided them, sliding past in the darkness. When he arrived near the long undulating wall which encircled the Muslim graveyard, he began calling Jungli in soft tones, glad that he had an excuse for entering the area of the tomb. The outer wall was easy to climb. Most of it had crumbled away. He leaped down among the gravestones, which stuck up like broken teeth in the tangled undergrowth. The dome towered above him, great and dark.

The drumming continued. It seemed to be everywhere. It rose up through the roots of the trees and trickled down through the creepers; it called from the graves and thudded somewhere below ground.

The walls of the dais on which the tomb rested towered ten or twelve feet above him. Nazakhat stumbled about, searching for the steps which would have taken him up, but they had been destroyed.

'Forgive me, forgive me,' he murmured touching a gravestone near the wall and reverently transmitting the touch with his fingers to his heart and head. He took off his sandals and placed them near the mound, then, bare-footed, he climbed on to the gravestone and stretched across the abyss to grip the top of the wall. For a moment, he hung in space, his toes groping for a hold in the damaged stones. Then he heaved himself up and over and dropped down before the entrance of the tomb.

He was sure he had made no sound, except for his panting breath and thudding heart, but the drumming came to an abrupt stop. There was a deathly silence. A single bird began to whistle sharply. He realised that a crack had appeared in the night sky and dawn was sliding through.

He crept forward trying to make out the steps which led to the tomb below. He wished he had brought a torch, for no light penetrated here. Feeling his way, he crept down, step by step, pausing on each step to listen. He heard nothing. He strained his eyes till they watered, and groped his way into the chamber. He sniffed the mouldy air and was sure there was a trace of marigolds and snuffed tallow lingering.

His foot hit something soft at the base of the tomb. With a cry, he stepped back and almost fell. A hand gripped his ankle. He yelled with terror. He stumbled backwards desperately trying to shake it off. He reeled on to the steps kicking and gasping and, in a kind of backstroke, with the thing still clutching his ankle, he fought his way up and threw himself out into the fresh air.

'You flaming idiot. Why did you have to go and shock me like that!' yelled Nazakhat, furious with relief when he saw it was Jungli. 'I could have hurt you. Kicked your teeth in or something. I thought you were attacking me.' Then Nazakhat giggled with relief at the sight of the tightly curled-up body of the wild child. Still asleep, he had entwined his arms through Nazakhat's legs and refused to wake up. 'Oh well. Let's get you home,' he shrugged, realising that no one, not even Jungli appeared to have witnessed his panic. He slung the child across his back and managed to drop back over the wall and down among the gravestones. The lanes were empty again.

Safely in their room, Nazakhat dumped the wild child back on to his bed. With an animal-like groan, Jungli rolled over, still asleep, and stretched out an arm. His hand fell open, fingers loose.

'What have you got there?' sighed Nazakhat. Something sparkled between Jungli's fingers. Jungli didn't awake when Nazakhat took it. He spat on it and rubbed away the dirt. It was a single earring with a red stone surrounded with white beads. Rather bright and gaudy, he thought. He stared at it a while, rubbed it further and twisted it around in his hand. 'Cheap trash,' he muttered and returned it to Jungli's open palm.

7 Jungli's gift

The next morning, when Nazakhat went to join the milk queue, he was stared at rather hard, then cold-shouldered. The conversation, which had been about the identity of the nocturnal drummer at the Muslim tomb, halted conspicuously at his arrival and Nazakhat knew they suspected him.

'Up in the night, were you?' asked the milkman's wife snidely, as she measured two pints of warm, fresh, buffalo milk into his container.

'Yes – but I was looking for Jungli. It was a full moon last night and . . .'

'Huh!' snorted a woman in line who'd overheard. 'So a drum was beating all by itself, was it?'

'You think it was me drumming, do you?' exclaimed Nazakhat.

'Who else? You're the only . . .' a man's voice trailed away to the word 'Mussalman' and Nazakhat knew that the man had only changed his epithet at the last minute. Instead of Mussalman he would probably have said pig-dog or some other obscenity to describe a hated Muslim.

'Perhaps someone's some back. People do; looking for belongings or just to glimpse their old homes,' suggested Nazakhat.

The people in the queue mumbled disparagingly and ignored him.

Nazakhat took the milk, his ears burning with fury, and stormed back to the school.

'They think it was me,' he cried despairingly to the old aunt.

'And it wasn't. Was it?' she asked, her head cocked to one side, her eye fixing him like a nail.

'Would I be so mad?' Nazakhat's voice rose in dismay. 'Wouldn't it be stirring up trouble? Why would I want to do that?'

'Well then, get on with you and put out the blackboard. The children are already coming in,' said Aunt, breaking out into a rare smile so that Nazakhat regretted all the mean things he had ever said about her in the past.

Bahadur was worried. Nazakhat was the only Muslim round here now. Surely he wouldn't do something like that? Now all Muslims were dead or driven out of the village except for Nazakhat. Orphaned and abandoned, he had lived wild with other bands of orphaned boys, until the schoolmaster had taken him under his protection. Bahadur often wondered what went on inside Nazakhat's head. When Jaspal came back, the two boys resumed their friendship as if nothing had happened. Even though Muslims had killed so many of Jaspal's family at least his parents and sister had survived. The Sikhs had killed every one of Nazakhat's family.

Nazakhat set out the blackboard under the shade of the mango tree, the pores of his skin prickling as if they could hear all the speculation around him. Trickles of children were turning up for school, converging from all directions across the fields. They sat cross-legged under the neem tree with their slates on their knees.

Marvinder arrived with her violin. The schoolmaster was pleased. Because she could read and write he had given her a job helping the little ones with their reading. Marvinder would take the very smallest ones aside and, in their own group, teach them the Hindi alphabet and their tables. When they had had enough of sitting and memorising, Marvinder would teach them games and dances, and laughter would ring out and she would roll around as if she were a child herself. It sent Jungli mad with delight and he would join in by hurling himself around wildly.

As Marvinder approached the schoolhouse, she heard shouts. She broke into a run. They were dressing Jungli. The schoolmaster's aunt had already put Jungli's bowl of milk out on the low verandah table and, seeing it, he struggled free and hurtled towards it. He would have plunged his face into the milk and lapped it like an animal, but Nazakhat was right there to pull him back.

'Oh no you don't. First we dry you, then you put on clothes.' He ducked the thrashing limbs and tried to steady Jungli while Aunt held up a shirt. But even after a year of living with the schoolmaster and his aunt, Jungli loathed clothes on his body. He fought and kicked and tried to escape, but he knew, in the end, that if he didn't wear his clothes he would not get his milk. So, having made his gesture, he suddenly went limp and Nazakhat finished dressing him.

Jungli dived nose first into the milk. Why did they bother dressing him? Milk splattered all over the front of his shirt.

'No, no, no! Naughty boy. Pick it up, Jungli. Hands. Hands.'

At the sight of Marvinder, the wild child hurtled towards her and flung himself, arms and legs, round her waist. Nazakhat grinned with relief to see Marvinder. 'I'm glad you've come. Now you can take over.'

Marvinder unfastened Jungli's arms from her waist and took his hand. 'What shall we learn today, Jungli?'

'Eee, eee, eeeee!' cried Jungli, trying to imitate Marvinder's violin. He hammered his fingers on the violin case.

'First some talking, then violin,' insisted Marvinder.

Marvinder had given herself the task of teaching Jungli to speak. Of all of them, Marvinder was the one who succeeded in making progress with him. The schoolmaster observed her concentration as she tried to break through the confusion of the wild boy's mind. She could be fiercely firm, able to quell his jerking movements and quieten his unstill body. She could grip both his hands and say a word over and over and suddenly, the boy would shock them and, without warning, repeat the word. Then she would hug him shouting, 'Yes, yes, yes!' When she played the violin it had an extraordinary effect on Jungli. He would leap about emitting strange squeals and howls as if he were attempting to join in. Spurred on, she would play faster and pull the strings and make strange sounds on her fiddle; and she would laugh and he would laugh – a gurgling, screaming laugh – and they would egg each other on with high-pitched grunts and squeals.

Sometimes Aunt would declare that Marvinder was becoming wild rather than Jungli civilised.

Jungli's bony fingers pulled open Marvinder's hand. She felt a small object pushed into it. When she looked down she saw the earring.

'Where did you get this, Jungli?' She looked at it more closely. 'It's very pretty.'

'Sssssssss . . .' hissed Jungli, bounding about on all fours.

Marvinder examined the earring. 'Do you think it's real?' She showed it to Nazakhat.

'Of course not!' Nazakhat shook his head with certainty. 'Jungli picked it up somewhere – perhaps at the old Muslim tomb. I had to go out again last night looking for him, and that's where I found him. By the way . . .' he said shyly. 'Did you hear the drumming last night? I thought it came from the tomb. That's why I went there when I was looking for Jungli.'

'And . . . ?' Marvinder urged him on. 'It wasn't you?'

'Not you too,' wailed Nazakhat. 'Doesn't anyone believe me?'

'Yes, yes, of course I believe you. If you say you didn't do it, then you didn't. But . . . who did?'

They stared at each other blankly.

'I didn't see anyone. Just Jungli – he scared the wits out of me, because he had gone right down into the tomb. That's where he must have picked up the earring.'

'It's very pretty. Almost good enough for a bride,' murmured Marvinder.

'It's just a bit of junk. Not worth more than a few annas if you ask me,' Nazakhat declared with certainty. 'I mean, it couldn't be real – not round these parts. Even before partition, there was no one that wealthy round here.'

'It looks so real. The stones look like rubies – and surely those are pearls.' Marvinder examined it closely.

'No such luck, you can be sure of that,' asserted Nazakhat.

'But real or not, it must have belonged to someone.' Marvinder held the earring to her ear dreamily.

'Anyway, it's yours now – Jungli found it. Finders keepers – and now he's given it to you. Why don't you put it on a chain and wear it round your neck? That would look nice.'

'Or,' suggested Marvinder, 'we could go back to the tomb and see if we can find the other one.' She smiled as if she knew she was half joking, then she said more seriously, 'If it wasn't you drumming last night, who was it?'

'I just don't know. Is someone trying to make trouble? I found Jungli there – but he didn't have a drum. Could Jungli beat a drum like that?'

'Jungli! Oh, no! No.' Marvinder was sure not. 'He would beat it wildly, without rhythm or awareness. Last night was different. It was real, like all those years ago when Mohammed Ali Khan used to guard the tomb. His drumming was like the sound of rain, or the wind hammering the autumn leaves. Nazakhat, bhai, you will be careful, won't you?'

'Me? Careful? I told you, Marvinder, it wasn't me.'

'Then who? Only a Muslim would beat the drum. Who else is there? Jungli, do you know?' asked Marvinder.

The wild child dropped to all fours and bared his teeth. He snarled a whistling kind of snarl. Something of a growl and something of a hiss and bounded away.

The schoolmaster's aunt took up a stick. It was time for lessons to begin. She began rattling the great metal triangle with all her might.

The question remained unanswered.

8   The nihang

Jaspal had left home early. Supposedly to go to school. It was only because Jhoti had begged him. 'For my sake, Jaspal. Just to keep your father happy. Please go to school. After all, it's only for a little while longer – then you'll have a qualification and be your own man.'

So he put on his school uniform – sky blue turban, white shirt and black trousers – and he stood on the long white road which ran past his village and waited for the bus. It was not what he wanted to do. It was not where he wanted to be. He often asked himself where he would be and what he would be doing if he had the choice, but he could never decide.

In England, he had thought he wanted more than anything to be back on the land; be with the other boys from his village working the fields, ploughing, seeding, watering and harvesting. It was coming up for harvesting the sugar-cane right now. Soon the air would reek of sugar when they cut the sugar-cane. But Jaspal knew he wouldn't be among them.

Nothing was as he thought it would be. An old anger burned inside him like a low fire, but he didn't know why. He kicked out at a stone in the road and sent it spinning into the ditch, and waited for the bus. He would make up his mind when he got into town. Would he bother with school or go to the cinema? He didn't care if his father beat him again.

His eye fixed on a speck of a man in the distance loping towards him along the dusty edge of the road. He looked like a strange flamingo with his thin, stick legs protruding from beneath a calf-length, faded-pink tunic. As he came closer, Jaspal noted the turban from which the sun had sucked out all but the faintest tinge of pink. It bristled with silver emblems and badges. Double leather straps crossed over his chest, fitted with fifty or more bullets for the rifle, which was slung across his back, and a holster for the knife hung at his waist. His walking-stick, which towered above him, doubled as a long home-made spear, hacked from a length of bamboo and topped with a sharpened, arrow-shaped, metal tip the size of a man's hand. He walked with a limp, yet with a regular rhythm which brought him inexorably nearer and nearer.

By now, Jaspal could see the man was an old nihang – a wandering holy man. Nihangs were known for their war-like philosophies and their partiality to bhang, a home brew. Jaspal looked around and wished there were others waiting for the bus. Such characters were a common enough sight, but they could be eccentric and unpredictable, often breaking into drunken quarrels and fights.

The gap between them closed. Jaspal could now see the detail of the nihang's ravaged, scarred face and his narrow but glittering eyes. His long, tangled, grey beard fell down his chest almost to his waist.

They eyed each other like two combatants. Jaspal stood his ground as the old man made straight for him. It dawned on Jaspal that he wouldn't go round him and, to avoid a collision, it was Jaspal who had to step aside.

The man passed with his eyes never leaving Jaspal. After a few paces he stopped. 'Eh! Have you got a drink in that bag of yours?'

'Yes, sir! I have some milk and paratha. You are welcome to it,' Jaspal answered politely. He opened up his schoolbag, and the warrior retraced his steps.

A cloud of dust on the horizon heralded the imminent arrival of the bus. The old man took the metal container with the milk in both hands. He tipped his head back and, without his lips touching the rim, poured the liquid into his open mouth. Then he helped himself to a paratha, grinding on the three or four teeth left in his mouth.

The bus arrived with its horn blasting. Jaspal stretched out a hand to retrieve his milk and parathas from the nihang, but the old man moved back and carried on eating and drinking.

'Sir!' cried Jaspal. 'I'm sorry, sir, but I must catch this bus. Keep a paratha, but please may I have back the container?'

The nihang could have been stone deaf for all the response he gave. He just carried on tipping the milk into his mouth and chewing on the parathas.

'Come on, if you're coming! Can't wait all day. Give the lad his food, you old cadger!' yelled the bus conductor disrespectfully.

The nihang dropped down on his haunches with no intention of complying.

'Get on, get on!' yelled other passengers. 'You're making us late.'

Jaspal shrugged. 'I'll catch the next,' he said, so the bus revved up and sped away, churning up the white dust.

Jaspal stood before the old man whose jaws still rotated on the paratha. 'Now I'll be late for school,' he said accusingly.

'Eh! School! What rubbish do they teach you there?' snorted the nihang between mouthfuls. 'English medium, is it?'

'Yes.'

The nihang spat to one side in disgust.

'Traitor!'

'What? Me?' asked Jaspal.

'Yes, you. What do you think, learning the tongue of our oppressors? If you learn the language of the oppressor then you will think as they do and you might just as well be one of them. But I tell you this, I would rather put my spear through your guts than have you learn their stinking language and become one of them.'

Jaspal leaped aside as the old man lunged his spear at him.

'Why can't I learn their language and yet not become one of them? What makes you think I can't use English to my own advantage?' he yelled from a distance.

The old nihang gulped down the last of the milk and tossed the container to Jaspal who had just seen his midday meal consumed in a flash.

'Because words make meaning. If you speak English then you think English and you understand in an English way.' He spat again adding, 'And I would never trust you. If you speak Punjabi, you will think Punjabi and understand in a Punjabi way and I would trust you with my life. Destroy a language and you destroy that spirit. See what I mean? It is what power is all about. That's why the Moguls banned the speaking of Punjabi when they ruled and repressed our homeland three hundred years ago. Muslims, English – they were all the same. We Punjabis have always had to fight our own corner. That's why I spit on your English. You think because the Britishers have gone we have won our war? No, I tell you. Every time you utter an English word, you aim a bullet at our people.'

The old nihang fumbled in his pockets and brought out a box of matches and a half-smoked cheroot of bhang leaves. He lit the end and began to puff on it. Jaspal watched him silently, wishing another bus would come. He vowed that, this time, nothing would stop him getting on it. After a while, the nihang offered it to Jaspal with a curt nod, and commanded him to smoke it. Jaspal accepted warily not wanting to upset the old warrior in any way. You never knew what substances went into these rolled-up leaves.

'Go on, go on! It won't kill you!' sneered the old man.

While Jaspal sucked and puffed, hating the strong, bitter flavour which filled his mouth and lungs, the nihang got to his feet. Jaspal handed him back his cheroot and retrieved his empty food tins which he packed back into his satchel. He looked up the empty road. No sign of a bus yet.

'You'd learn more walking with me,' muttered the nihang, 'instead of going to the school of our enemies. Walk with me, lad and I'll tell you things which they'll never tell you in any school.'

Behind him, Jaspal heard the bus roaring down the road, its klaxon blaring. The old nihang's bony fingers gripped his elbow. Jaspal stiffened for a moment as he prepared to struggle free. Why should he let a crazy old man control him like this? He looked into his face. The lines were scored across his parched skin like dried-up rivers. Only his eyes gleamed dark and liquid deep. Suddenly, it no longer seemed important to try and escape. He didn't even turn, as the bus swept past, annihilating them for a while in a fine cloud of white dust, and he allowed himself to be propelled along the road towards the city.

9 Commitments

It was already late afternoon when Jaspal and the nihang arrived on the outskirts of the city. Jaspal was painfully hungry. Even though odd passers-by on the wayside had dropped food or money into the nihang's begging bowl, the old man hadn't shared any of it with Jaspal. Jaspal felt bitter. After all, he had given him all his food. He looked at the old man with disgust and said, 'Well, I'm going off now to find something to eat. I'm starving.'

'You, starving?' the old man cackled. 'Look at you!' He squeezed the flesh of Jaspal's upper arm, and then his cheeks, while Jaspal flinched with the pain. 'Look at this fat! There's nothing starving about you. Why, if I chose to eat you, you'd last me a month! Feel my arm – go on!' He grabbed Jaspal who shrank away repelled. 'Squeeze it, squeeze it!' He forced Jaspal's hand to his upper arm.

Squeamishly, Jaspal tried to grip some of the ancient flesh

between his fingers, but got mostly tendon and bone.

'See?' sneered the old man. 'There's nothing there, is there? You're not starving. I'm the one who's starving. So stop being such a namby-pamby. Your stomach could do with some shrinking. A little bit of hunger won't hurt you. Here, carry my spear for me. I'm feeling its weight.'

Jaspal took the spear which rose above him twice his height. It was surprisingly heavy. He liked it. It was the first time he had held a spear. He lifted it to shoulder height and aimed it in front of him. 'Can I try to throw it?' he asked.

'Do what you like,' sniffed the old man, dropping down to his haunches to eat a paratha which had been dropped into his bowl by a passer-by.

Jaspal swung the spear back and forth and back and forth, then hurled it with all his might. How humiliating then, that it had barely left his hand before it was already thudding flat to the ground.

The old man rocked with derision. 'Pathetic!' he sneered.

Jaspal picked up the spear with a scowl, furious at being made fun of. He held the spear up again and, with extra energy because of his anger, thrust it into flight. This time, it stayed airborne a fraction of a second longer, but still landed flat instead of point first.

'Not like that, you idiot. I can see you're going to need lessons. Look!' He thrust the last piece of paratha into his mouth and stood up. 'Give it here,' he said impatiently.

Jaspal handed over the spear. Surely the old man wouldn't do much better. He was such a scarecrow of a fellow and held the spear like a woman with a broom. The nihang gripped the bamboo stem, straightened his body – and in a sudden swift movement like the attack of a snake, he uncoiled his arm and the spear left his hand like an arrow from a bow. It arched through the air ten, eleven maybe twelve feet, and plunged point first into the earth quivering with the force.

'Phew!' Jaspal blew his cheeks with respect.

'That's me when I wasn't even trying,' cackled the old man seeing the boy's astonishment. 'Stick with me, lad and I'll teach you more than just how to throw a spear.'

They entered the city and headed for the Golden Temple. Jaspal really did feel weak with hunger now. He didn't care what the old nihang said, he abandoned him and made for the free kitchen to get a hand-out of paratha and a mug of butter milk.

His stomach full at last, Jaspal curled up, suddenly over-whelmed with exhaustion. He was just giving into sleep when a piercing yell – 'Oi! You!' – and a kick in his back, put paid to any such idea. He jerked to his feet.

'I wondered where you'd got to.' The old nihang stood swaying in front of him, his spear in one hand and a bottle in the other. Whatever was in the bottle, it wasn't the orangeade that it said on the label. He took a swig from the bottle and sat down beside the boy. At first Jaspal was repelled by the stench of alcohol and he tried, respectfully, to edge away. But a claw-like hand gripped him. 'Eh, boy. Here, have a swig of this. It will make a man of you.' He thrust the bottle in his face. Jaspal made a token gesture of tossing back a gulp, and tried again to move away, but the old man held him fast.

Jaspal tipped the bottle above his mouth and gulped down something so burning, he immediately doubled over spluttering and choking.

The old man rocked with laughter and slid his back down a pillar to a sitting position next to the boy. His spear fell to his side. 'Oh, dear, oh, dear, you have a lot to learn, eh?'

'Come on, man!' came a stern voice. 'You know we don't allow alcohol on the premises. Go on, don't desecrate this place any longer. You should be ashamed at setting such a bad example to this young lad. Oh, it's you.'

Jaspal recognised Amarjit Singh, the same guardian warrior who had watched him bathe the last time he was at the Golden Temple.

'I'm sorry to see you in such bad company. Does your father know?'

Jaspal shrugged resentfully.

'Do you think I don't remember you? You have brains. You read from the scriptures perfectly. We have watched you before and had hopes for you. We need young men like you. So why waste yourself with a drunken nihang? He is a disgrace to his religion. I think of you sometimes, and think what excellent training you would get if you went to a taksal. There, you could train to be a priest. It is where you should be.'

Jaspal said nothing.

The guardian waved a fierce hand at the nihang. 'Well then, help this old man out of here if you are his disciple.'

'Oh no, sir! It's nothing like that,' cried Jaspal. 'I just met him on the road.'

Jaspal was so ashamed he wanted to dissociate himself from the nihang. He tried to move away as if he had some other task of his own, but the guardian gestured firmly. 'Help him out,' he said. Jaspal could see that the nihang was too drunk to cope alone, so he picked up the spear and put out a hand for the nihang to grasp. Still clutching his bottle, the old man slung an arm round Jaspal's neck and they both staggered up the steps. At the top of the steps, Jaspal looked back. The guardian was still there, watching them. Jaspal wanted to speak; to explain.

The guardian stared at him with narrowed eyes, then beckoned him. Jaspal propped the old man against a pillar and came back down the steps to the guardian warrior. 'We could do with young blood like you,' he said in a low, intense voice. 'You look like someone with guts; someone prepared to take chances; make sacrifices. Don't waste yourself on stupid old men like that. Take my advice. Go to the Baba Deep Singh taksal. Ask for me, Amarjit Singh. If it's one thing I promise you, I'll make a warrior out of you – a warrior to fight the cause.'

'What cause?' asked Jaspal.

'You see how much you have to learn. You don't know the cause, or who you are or why you are here. Till you learn those things, you'll never amount to anything. You'll either end up a drunk like him – or a soft, conniving useless creature, whose very existence would be worse than a traitor's.' He gave Jaspal a push which sent him pounding back up the steps.

For some moments they stood in the road, the nihang swaying about, uncertain which way to go. He held Jaspal's arm in a grip which almost stopped the flow of his blood. Jaspal tried to shake himself free. He wanted to get away; he wanted to think. Instead, he found himself steered across the road to a low wall below some shops. Here the old man slumped down to the ground pulling Jaspal with him.

The nihang emptied the rest of the bottle into his mouth and leaned his head back against the wall. He closed his eyes and began to breathe very deeply and loudly. After a while, his jaw relaxed and his mouth fell open. Slowly, slowly, the grip on Jaspal's arm weakened and finally gave way. Jaspal edged himself out of reach and was just getting to his feet, when a hand shot out again and grabbed him.

'I must go,' said Jaspal desperately. 'My dad'll kill me for being so late.' But the old man's hand held him fast.

'No, no, no! Not yet.' His eyes opened and fixed themselves

on him. 'I haven't finished with you yet. Your father won't object to you helping a holy man. It is your duty. Tell that father of yours, tell him to send you to the gurudwara. Let the priests teach you. You must learn to be a Sikh – a Punjabi; uphold your heritage, religion and homeland. Remember what Guru Gobind Singh said? "The sparrow must learn to fight like the hawk." You must learn bravery; learn the martial arts. You never know who will turn out to be your enemy. You never know when it might be required of you to be a martyr – like those of us who were in that garden there–' He pointed down the road to the narrow alley leading to the Jallianwallah Bagh Gardens. 'I was there, you know.'

'You?' Jaspal echoed disbelievingly. Jaspal knew what he was referring to. There couldn't be a man, woman or child in the Punjab who didn't know about the Amritsar Massacre even though it happened over thirty years ago. But Jaspal thought the nihang was boasting. The man was nothing but a drunken liar.

The nihang saw Jaspal's face. He yanked him to the ground and pulled his face so close to his that Jaspal felt the rough beard on his cheek. 'You don't believe me, eh?'

'Yes, yes, I do. It must have been awful!' stammered Jaspal.

'Awful? You bet it was awful. *It* was cold-blooded murder. *It* killed my father. *It* killed hundreds of innocent people. I only survived because of the bodies which fell on top of me.'

'You mean you were actually there when the British opened fire?' Jaspal began to think perhaps the man wasn't lying after all. 'What was it like?' He tried to sound reasonable and interested in the hope he would be released from that grip.

'I was a young man – about your age. 1919 – that was the year. Remember it.' The old nihang leaned forward on his spear, his eyes half closed, but his fingers enclosing Jaspal's wrist like a manacle. 'It was a peaceful demonstration. Peaceful, I tell you. No one came for violence. Men brought their women and children with them. I came with my father and brothers. We just wanted to tell the British how we felt. We were many though – hundreds of us – perhaps too many for that walled garden with only one narrow path to come or go.' He nodded his head in the direction of a narrow dark lane which Jaspal could see over the road. 'Yes! We trapped ourselves as surely as goats for the slaughter.'

'Why were you there? What did you want?' asked Jaspal.

'Justice!' hissed the old man. 'Justice. Had we not gone in thousands to fight for the British in Europe and Africa during that first world war? There was not a soldier on this planet more brave than we Sikhs, I tell you. No German, no Britisher, no South African fakir could instil the kind of fear in the breast of the enemy that we could. We fought and we died. We fought again and again – and we died in our thousands. Loyal – I tell you; utterly loyal to our British masters – and they repaid us like dogs. Why, worse than dogs. The English love their dogs. But us – us – suddenly, when the war was over, and they were victorious, we were just brown-skinned scum. We expected to be rewarded for helping them win the war, as other soldiers were rewarded: pensions for the wounded; help for those returning. And we expected rights: liberty to practise our own laws and religion, run our temples and speak our own language. But instead, they repressed us, humiliated us and made us crawl on our bellies. Some of us who had been officers crawled on our bellies before tinpot Tommies who spat on us. They won't teach you that in your English medium school.' The old man's hatred dribbled from his mouth. 'We were a peaceful protest, I tell you, peaceful; satyagraha – peaceful action. Gandhi's way, though he had already been arrested, but still we did it his way. Like children we stood there unarmed and still they sent in troops as if we were wild animals.'

Jaspal listened and felt anger rise in his guts too. He could picture it all; feel as they must have felt.

'That General Dyer – may he burn in hell – how he must have hated us. When we stood before him, he didn't see humans, he saw vermin. He blocked the only exit with his armed trucks and sent in soldiers with rifles.

'We weren't prepared. We were innocent. We had come with our mothers and fathers – whole families. They gave us no warning. All we did was shout for our rights – and, without warning, they opened fire. Pphtt!' The old man flicked his palm as if tossing off a fly. 'That's all we were. Flies to be swatted. We died – hundreds of us. The dead, like my father and brothers, fell on the rest of us, and protected us, though hundreds more were wounded.'

'And to think my father went and fought for the British in the next world war,' said Jaspal, shaking his head disbelievingly.

'Schrr! Not me,' snarled the old man. 'I joined Subhash Chandra Bose in Malaya – he was a true patriot. When the British were recruiting us into the army to fight against Hitler and fight against the Japanese, Bose asked, "Why should we fight our enemy's enemy?" I could not answer him. Why should we be cannon fodder for our repressers, indeed, especially after last time? So I joined him over the border. We set up our own regiment and fought against the British alongside the Japanese. We lost the war, but I regained my pride.'

'And now?' asked Jaspal. 'The British have gone. We're all right now, aren't we?'

'All right now! Hah!' The old man broke into a cackling which turned into a coughing fit, and Jaspal had to beat the old man's back. 'Now! Oh, oh now! We have just as many enemies. What did they do, our enemy, but divide us up and create more enemies within? We're fools to have let it happen. Wasn't that always the British way – the way of all rulers – divide and rule? We were as much betrayed by our own politicians as we were by the British. And why? Because our leaders were educated the English way; they spoke English and thought English and did things the English way – that's our leaders for you. Poor Punjab, poor Punjab. Split up like any old robber's booty; a chunk to the Muslims, the rest to the Hindus and what about us – eh? What about the Sikhs? Nothing for us.' He spat and took another swig from the bottle. His eyes rolled upwards and he swayed. Jaspal thought he would fall into a dead sleep, but, suddenly, those glittering eyes opened and fixed themselves on him. 'Boy! Boy! You can see – I'm old. I've fought my battles; I've killed – many people – I've killed our enemies – yes, British too. I could have been hanged, but they never caught me. I was too clever. "The sparrow must learn to fight like the hawk!" Well, I did. I fought like a hawk and tore many an enemy limb from limb. But the enemy is like Ravana, the ten-headed King of the Demons. You strike off one head and another grows in its place. We Sikhs were born out of conflict. It is our sacred duty to fight. Now you. What about you? What are you going to do about our enemies, eh, boy? You're going to fight, aren't you? I can see it in your eyes. You have anger in your belly too. Eh, boy? Will you fight, to get it all back? Our language, our rights. If the Muslims have Pakistan and the Hindus have India, why should we not have Khalistan, eh? Why should we not have back our old kingdom? Why should any other people rule us?' He dragged himself to his feet and thrust his spear into the air. 'Khalistan!' he yelled drunkenly. Then, as if pole-axed, he fell to his knees and collapsed headlong on to his bundle.

Free at last, Jaspal stood unable to move, stunned by the old man's tirade. He gazed at the ancient body lying in the dust; an obscure warrior, forgotten by time. With sudden tenderness, Jaspal undid the old man's bundle, extricated a piece of sheet and gently covered the nihang's body from the night. The rest of the bundle, he pillowed under the old man's head. Then Jaspal fled away through the night like an escaping slave.

Jaspal had walked most of the way home along the railway tracks. But, when a single engine came chugging along, he hailed it and the driver slowed sufficiently so Jaspal could hitch a lift for the five or so miles left. But it didn't make any difference to his father's anger.

'Where the hell have you been?' Govind's shadow was swinging with fury as he rocked to and fro on his heels beneath the kerosene lamp.

Jaspal stared at his father, unmoved. He knew that after the shouting would come the beating. He must just take it as best he could.

'You weren't at school today, so you needn't lie about that,' his father roared. 'And for once, you weren't with that Muslim good-for-nothing layabout, Nazakhat.'

'That Muslim good-for-nothing, as you call him, saved

our lives while you were . . .' *in England, abandoning your family, betraying our mother, marrying another woman, committing crimes and going to prison . . .* Jaspal struggled to keep back the bitter accusations he wanted to hurl at his father.

'What have you been up to? Don't you care about your mother? Didn't she beg you to go to school? Have you no regard, even for her, if you choose to disobey me?'

That hurt. He did have regard for Jhoti. He loved her, but . . .

'What kind of a son are you? Disrespectful to your parents, irresponsible. I've been hearing about you. Going into the bazaars and to the cinema; mixing with God knows what kind of villains. Playing truant and coming home at all hours of the day or night. What are you learning from all of this, I ask you? What am I to say to Harold Chadwick? Every month he sends money for your education. What do I tell him when you fail to get your leaving certificate? For fail you will.'

Till that moment, Jaspal had stood with bowed head, taking his father's anger. But at the mention of Harold Chadwick – an Englishman, a colonialist, one of those who had ruled India – he remembered what the nihang had told him and his blood boiled. 'How can you take money from that imperialist Britisher?' snarled Jaspal. 'How can you let him continue to treat us as inferiors who need patting on the head like children and given hand-outs as if we are beggars? Have you no pride?'

'Why, you insolent devil!' Govind leaped down from the verandah yelling and shouting at the top of his voice, lashing out at the boy with his stick. The sound of stick on body and the involuntary grunts and cries, which escaped from between Jaspal's clenched teeth, brought his mother and sister rushing out.

'Stop, please stop!' begged Jhoti, trying to throw herself between Jaspal and his father's stick. Blows landed on her, and on Marvinder, who in horror had leaped down to protect her mother and brother.

'I don't want to go to an English language school any more! I'm going to be a real Sikh. I wish to join a gurudwara. I want to learn the scriptures and to read the Guru Granth Sahib.'

Jaspal shocked even himself. As Govind froze, stick in hand, Jaspal wondered whether he had meant the words which came out of his mouth.

Suddenly, there was a great calm. Govind lowered his stick and Jhoti and her daughter moved to each other's side. 'Perhaps that is the best thing for you, especially now that Marvinder is to marry.'

'Marry?' The word fell like a bombshell. 'You, Marvinder? Marry? Has he found you a husband? Who is it? How much is he selling you for?' He stared desperately at her. Marvinder was more beloved to him than anyone. Even his mother. It was she who had guided and protected him through the worst of their nightmares. He couldn't bear it when she was mocked and jeered at by those ignorant villagers, so that no family had made offers for her for their precious sons. Even little children threw stones at her and called her names, and often he had chased them off, threatening to tear them apart if they didn't leave her alone.

'Who have you sold her to?' Jaspal's voice was leaden with rage.

Govind looked his son in the eye. He seemed suddenly weary. 'Why do you use such language? We have come back here to live in our village with our own people. Why should we behave differently from them? This isn't England. You made a free choice to come back. Go. Join the priests,' said Govind bitterly, 'and let us get on with our own lives.'

'Son, we have not sold her, that is not a good way to speak.' Jhoti came and put an arm round his shoulders. 'This is a good man — and he asks for no dowry. You know him well, doesn't he, daughter?'

Marvinder nodded and lifted an arm to hide her desperate face. Then Jaspal saw it, encircling her arm: the band of gold; the bracelet.

10 Last star

I am Jhoti. I am the daughter of Harbans Singh, wife of Govind Singh and mother of Jaspal Singh. I have a daughter, Marvinder.

Without a man a woman is nothing. If her father dies she needs an uncle. If her husband dies she needs a son. If her son dies she needs a nephew or a cousin, or any relative so long as it is a male. A woman is not fit for independence. This is Manu's Law.

But during the time that the laws of the land collapsed and families were split asunder, I lived without the help of any man. For more than two years, when the fields burned and the rivers ran red, when the ogres of the night took over the day and the natural order of things was turned upside down, I survived without my husband or my brothers or my son.

I have a daughter. No one has yet asked to marry her. If she doesn't marry she will be a burden on her father. When her father dies she will be a burden on her brother. When her brother dies she will be a burden on his son.

When I lived in the jungle, I was a burden to no man.

Yes, Bahadur called last week with his suggestion. I didn't tell my daughter straight away. How could I tell Marvinder that a man older than her father wished to marry her? 'Let her have a few more days in innocence,' I begged my husband. But he said we couldn't afford to be sentimental.

I am always the first to wake. Even when I lived in the forest, I awoke before the birds, before the last star had faded from the sky.

I still check that my family is here with me. Although it is a year since we were all reunited, I have to be sure it is not all a dream, that the nightmare of death and massacre and separation is really over.

The morning of Bahadur's visit, I checked as usual. I made sure that Jaspal was in his bed – and then – Marvinder. Often I just stand over them as they sleep, and marvel that they are alive. 'Thank you God. Thank you, thank you.'

But this morning I was full of dread as I stood by her bed. How was I going to tell Marvinder that the schoolmaster had proposed marriage and that he was coming round today to discuss it? I know she's fifteen. I was already married by thirteen and had Marvinder before I was fifteen, but, to me, she's still my baby. I lost more than two years of her life. I wasn't there to see her change from child to woman. I'm not ready to lose her and I know she doesn't want to marry yet. I said to Govind, my husband, when I heard about the proposal, 'But husband she's so young and he's so old.'

'What does age matter?' retorted Govind. 'She's a woman now. She's ready for marriage. Anyway, we can't pick and choose.'

87

It's true. We can't pick and choose. Since Marvinder returned from England she is different. England changed her, and it changed the way others think about her. They regard Marvinder as an outsider, a freak. Families keep apart from her as if she were contaminated, as if she might influence their daughters or seduce their sons. Travelling the roads, free, unchecked, beholden to no one, who knows where she has been, whose company she has kept, what might have polluted her, who might have touched her? She has crossed the ocean, lived among foreigners in England; learned new ways. She is different now. In the whole year that she has been home, no family has asked for her to be a wife to their son. She has become an alien in her own village. Shall I tell her what I know? What I learned about wandering free?

'Look on the good side,' says my husband. 'Bahadur Manmohan Singh is an educated man. He likes books and music as she does. That is why he has asked for her. He can see that she could work in the school. She would be an asset to him, for he needs more than an uneducated farmer's daughter at his side. And where would she find a better man, I ask you?'

'But he's even older than you!' I had wailed. 'Must she marry a man old enough to be her father?'

'What does age matter? What's more, he doesn't ask for any dowry. How many men are there round here who would not willingly bankrupt a girl's family for her dowry?'

He was right. I knew he was right. What could I do or say? I drew my veil across my face to hide my tears.

In a moment she will waken and I will tell her.

You see why daughters are considered such a burden from the minute they are born? Not only must their virtue be protected, but the expenditure required to get them married can leave a family in debt or bonded as slaves for generations to come. Not so long ago they might not have let me keep my first-born child, because she was female. Even so, within the hour of her birth, my mother-in-law suggested we follow the custom of placing my girl-baby in an earthen vessel with a morsel of cane sugar, and burying her beneath the ground.

'Then you must bury me with her!' I had shrieked when I overheard her whispering. My screams of horror embarrassed them. The English lived nearby at the time, and my in-laws feared they might hear about it and bring in the officials. So, cursing me heartily – and my infant daughter – they dropped the idea. It took a long time before I was able to conceive again. Thank God it was a son. I might not have succeeded in saving another daughter.

When her mother had told her, Marvinder had instantly gasped in anguish. 'No. Not yet. Please, Ma. Don't make me. I'm not ready. And I don't want to marry him. In England, girls and boys choose for themselves and no one marries until they want to.'

'But daughter,' whispered Jhoti sadly, 'you are not in England. You are home where you belong and where you must live as everyone else lives.'

Bahadur Manmohan Singh had arrived on a bicycle. He looked pristine in pure white kurta pyjamas and a pale green turban. Marvinder watched him secretly from the roof.

Marvinder felt numb as she saw him carefully raise his bicycle up on to its stand and unloop the cloth bag which had hung from the handlebars. He walked up the verandah steps and slipped out of his chappals before proceeding further, barefooted.

'Ah! Bahadur Singh! Welcome, welcome!' Govind went out on to the verandah to greet him profusely. Each clasped his hands together in a deep namaste, then Govind held aside the bamboo blind and ushered the schoolmaster inside.

Marvinder heard no more.

She had to get away. She crept down the verandah steps and fled towards the palace.

'Why must I marry? Give me one good reason why?' she called through the echoing rooms.

The watcher shrank out of sight into an alcove as Marvinder rushed by, churning up the dust with her bare feet and disturbing the bats hanging from the ceilings. She took out Patrick's letter from her violin case and flopped down against the wall to read it. Nothing could prevent this marriage taking place, no matter what Patrick thought. She read the letter again, the tears sliding down her face. 'I hope they haven't married you off already,' he had said. Next time she wrote to him, she would have to say yes. She leaned her head back against the thick dusty wall.

It took her a while to control her emotion and hear a low singing coming from within the very wall itself. The voice rose and fell, sliding like water, over semi-tones and quarter-tones; low, smooth, comforting, as if it were trying to ease the pain inside her. She stopped crying and her breathing settled to a steady rhythm. She listened to the singing. Gradually, it died away to a whispering and murmuring, drifting away so softly that she did not hear the exact moment when the sound was no more.

Silence. Sleep. Dreaming. If she had asked herself, who was that? what was that? her answer would have been, don't ask. So she didn't.

After a while, she took out her violin and went up to the top terrace and played. She played and played; all the pieces she knew; just allowing the music and the reverberation of the wood against her cheek to stifle her anguish.

The schoolmaster, Bahadur Manmohan Singh, was returning home through the wilderness of the palace grounds after his interview with Govind. He heard the thin, high, quivering notes. He stopped and shaded his eyes against the sun and looked up through the tracery of weeds and creepers to the upper terrace of the palace. He knew it was Marvinder. He hoped to see her.

Her father Govind favoured the marriage: 'The sooner the better,' he had said, adding, 'I am deeply honoured that you enquire about my daughter. To be honest, Bahadur, I had already thought that she would be an ideal wife for you. You are an educated man, and need more than just an illiterate village girl. There must be educated girls in Amritsar or Lahore – but then, would they be prepared to live out here in a simple village? Would they have any interest in your school? Although city girls would come with considerable dowry, eh?' He had cocked his head sideways, wanting to hear Bahadur Manmohan Singh repeat that a dowry was not a condition of the marriage.

'I told you, sir. I don't require dowry. Indeed, I don't agree with dowry. I do not seek a commodity. I seek a wife.'

Govind had relaxed and there was a barely repressed sigh of relief. 'That is an excellent point of view. I am perfectly certain that my daughter could not find a better husband. We should fix the date. It's time she settled down. Her experiences through partition and England have made her headstrong and too independent. You'll have to be firm with her. So – when shall it be?'

As Bahadur stood listening to her, he wished he could go into the palace and ask her now, himself. But he knew he couldn't. Even though this was not entirely a traditional marriage, he must wait and do things in the proper manner. He carried on walking, while the watcher watched.

When Marvinder returned her violin to its case, she glanced

at her row of stones lying in order where she had left them. Red, grey, lighter grey, white – and – an earring – of red stones like rubies, and white stones like pearls. The small piece of jewellery stood in line with the stones. Her hand flew to her pocket. How come? How did Jungli's earring get there? Yet her fingers felt the earring Jungli had given her. It was in her pocket where she had put it. Wonderingly, she took it out and placed it next to the other. It was a perfect match.

She thought that somewhere behind her she heard the faintest sigh.

'Jungli?' Marvinder called out almost in a whisper. 'Jungli? Did you find the other one?'

There was no answer. She sighed. 'Well, thank you anyway,' she said, though she wasn't sure to whom she said it.

Marvinder didn't return home till she was sure Bahadur Singh had gone. Then she faced her father. 'I'm not ready to marry, Pa,' she said quietly.

He gave her a package which contained a gift from the schoolmaster. She took it but did not open it.

'Nonsense. You are more than ready, and it is my wish; the sooner the better. You will not get a better offer than this one.'

Marvinder looked at her mother. Jhoti wouldn't meet her gaze. She kept her eyes steadfastly lowered, staring at a red ant on the floor, which was dragging a leaf twice its size towards some destination of its own.

'Must it be straight away? Can't I wait a little longer?' she begged.

'How long?' retorted Govind.

'A year? Maybe two?' Even as she spoke, she knew it sounded ridiculous.

'Two years? You must be mad!' exploded her father. Jhoti knew this was a battle which could not be won.

'Why do you want to wait?' Govind was now ranting. 'What are you waiting for? What difference does it make if you marry next month or even next year? You are being selfish. It's not as though we have dozens of suitors lining up to marry you. And how lucky you are. He is a decent man; he comes from a good family. It is ridiculous for you to wait. I insist the marriage takes place as soon as possible.'

'Please, husband!' Jhoti falteringly touched her husband's arm. 'The girl has been through much suffering. Be patient, I beg you. Treat her gently.'

Govind halted his tirade. He strode from the room and out to the pump where he yanked the handle up and down as though he would pull it out of its socket. He thrust his face under the shoot of cold water and splashed it all over his head. Mother and daughter drew closer to each other and watched him in silence. Jhoti glanced anxiously at Marvinder. Her face was as still as death. Only her hands moved, rotating Bahadur's package. Govind came back; mother and daughter instinctively stepped apart and stood with eyes down.

'I will discuss everything with Bahadur Singh. We shall see how soon he wants the ceremony to take place. Perhaps he will be prepared to wait a little while – a month or two. But this I tell you: I will ask nothing that will make him withdraw his request for your hand. Now open the packet and see his gift so that I can convey your thanks to him.'

Marvinder had stared blankly at the gold bracelet. She had wanted to run down to the shore of the lake and hurl it as far out as she could into the waters. 'Put it on, girl. Put it on,' Govind ordered harshly.

Obediently, she had put it on.

11 Wishes like wild flowers

A beast lives in the palace. A beast with monstrous face and twisted body. Humans shy away from his ugliness and dogs bark furiously at the sight of him. By day he goes spying – moving invisibly, enveloped in his turban, which binds his face as well as his head. By night he emerges, stalking the wilderness gardens of the palace or wandering along the moon-reflecting shore of the lake. And when he sleeps? What does he dream of when he sleeps? Who has ever loved him? Does his heart beat like ours, yearn like ours, ache like ours? Is it part of him? Or is it a living thing in its own right – separate, pulsating, waiting to take control? A soul of a tortured creature? Can the soul of a beast know truth and beauty?

But his voice is like honey dripping from the hives which

hang among the palace eaves. He knew he could win her with his voice. So when she came to the palace, he sang to her, whispered to her, spoke in low tones so that she was never sure if it was the wind or the murmurings of insects or the scufflings of little animals; and he played games with her, adding to her collection of stones and leaving patterns for her to complete.

To begin with, she didn't ask. There seemed to be a presence within the very stones of the walls. She didn't know if it was of this world or another. She didn't want to know what or whom or why. All she knew was that she was not afraid.

But on the day of her betrothal, she came to the palace and leaned back against the wall which had become her friend and murmured, as if to her friend, 'I am to be married.'

'I know.' The voice sighed through the wall.

'It's not what I want.'

'I know that too.'

'I wish . . .'

'All young girls wish,' said the voice. 'Wishes are like wild flowers. They sprout up – they don't care where; in ditches and wastelands; in neglected gardens; in forests and wilder-nesses; in the cracks of walls and abandoned buildings. I am like a wish.'

'Who are you?' Marvinder never thought she would ever ask the question.

'Must you have an answer?'

She thought for a long time. Then she said, 'No. Not yet, anyway.'

The next time she came, she found a small posy of wild flowers lying within a circle of stones. She put it in her hair and felt like a goddess.

12 Knowing your enemies

Jaspal jumped a train and went into Amritsar and then searched the whole city. He asked, not just at the Golden Temple, but in gurudwaras outside the city and at tea houses along the main trunk roads leading out of the city, if anyone had seen his nihang. When night fell, he didn't stop, but moved from one glowing wayside fire to the next, braving the taunts and raucous jeers of wandering drunks and deranged wanderers scattered along the roadside, or in the vicinity of tea houses and drinking dens. He stared into the faces of old holy men, collapsed in sleep like discarded bundles of rags until, at last, Jaspal found him under a peepul tree on a small road leaving the city on the southside. He was snoring loudly and dead to the world.

The old nihang was still asleep well after dawn the next morning, and didn't awaken when a slight shadow fell across him. Jaspal carefully extricated the cooking pot from his bundle lying under his hand and brought it back brimming with fresh buffalo milk begged from a nearby farmer's wife. She didn't refuse Jaspal, for she recognised him as the disciple of a holy man. The boy looked earnest in his bright saffron turban and they had already seen him tending to the fire near the old man.

The old nihang woke up bad-tempered and hung-over. He glowered at Jaspal, who was adding bits of wood to the fire.

'And what the dickens are you doing on my patch, may I ask?' the nihang demanded, sitting up abruptly and clutching his head.

'The fire was almost out. I'm just bringing it back to life so I can brew up some tea,' said Jaspal.

'Oh you are, are you? And who, may I ask, said you could go sniffing round me and my belongings like a thief? Who said you could interfere with my fire?'

'I didn't need anyone to tell me that, if I didn't save the fire, you wouldn't be able to boil milk for tea until you had made another one, and that I could save you all the trouble by acting now,' Jaspal answered bold as brass.

The nihang made to get up and assert his authority but a violent pain seared through his head, and he fell back with a groan. 'All right, all right, clever dick. But don't think you can pull a fast one on me. What the devil are you doing here anyway? Why aren't you at that stinking school of yours, learning the devil's language?'

'You said you could teach me far more if I stayed with you. Well, I thought about it and decided you were right. I want to stay with you. I won't be a nuisance. I'll serve you; fetch and carry for you, be your disciple in exchange for learning your philosophies and skills. I want to learn to throw a spear like you.'

'Oh you do, do you?' snorted the old man, and spat vigorously. 'Why should you want to learn to throw a spear? Why not throw a stick or a ball? The spear is a weapon. The weapon is for fighting enemies. You don't even know who are your enemies!'

'I didn't before I met you. Now, I'm beginning to understand and I know you can show me,' persisted Jaspal.

'Why should I want some pip-squeak of a boy hanging round me, getting in the way? I know you boys: like magpies; you'll see something else glitter and be off. No staying power these days; no dedication. Anyway, what does your father have to say on the matter?'

Jaspal shrugged. 'Nothing much. He was fed up with beating me for not going to school. Anyway, he was pretty glad to be rid of me – just as he's got rid of my sister by marring her off to an old codger – oh, no disrespect,' he added hastily, as the old nihang raised a single eyebrow at the remark, 'but she's only fifteen and her husband is older than my father. It isn't right. It isn't fair.' Jaspal's voice rose with bitterness. 'If I had been older, I would have prevented it. I would have supported her myself until the right husband made an offer for her.'

'Yes, well. Just shows what a pip-squeak you are. What difference does it make? She's a woman – this sister of yours. So, young, old, fat, thin, rich, poor – a woman needs a husband, and if that was the best your father could get, then so be it. It's probably decreed in her stars. Why interfere or even have an opinion on the matter?'

Jaspal stared at the ground full of misery and uncertainty.

'Well, go on, make the tea then,' grunted the nihang, 'while I think about what to do with you over my washing.' He staggered over to the canal bank and slithered down the slope to the water. There came the sound of slapping and sloshing and groaning, with the cool of the water on bare body, and loud praying interspersed with gargling and spitting and the singing of hymns.

Bu the time he came back, rubbing himself down and combing out his hair, Jaspal had rigged up a spit and hung the metal pot of milk over the flame. Without speaking, the nihang indicated with a nod that in his cloth bundle lying nearby

Jaspal would find all the ingredients he needed to make chai: tea leaves, sugar, spices and herbs. Jaspal undid the knotted cloth and shook it out to find a number of tobacco tins which the old man was using as containers. Identifying the ingredients, he stirred them in with a stick, bringing the whole brew to a boil.

'Not bad,' muttered the old man, who had heaved himself into a squatting position, when Jaspal finally handed him a tin of steaming chai. He sucked noisily, trying to put some air between the burning liquid and his tongue.

'Right, you've earned yourself a day's instruction,' rasped the nihang. 'Get everything together now and let's get on the road.'

Jaspal was amazed how quickly the old nihang was transformed from a shambling tramp to a nimble, goat-like creature, loping along so fast, limp and all. Jaspal had to stride out to keep up with him. It was a while, before he realised what direction they were going in.

On the outskirts of Deri the nihang just muttered in a voice which did not allow argument: 'Go home, boy. Do not betray the father. Go forward with consent.'

13 Knowing your friends

Another letter came for Marvinder. This time it was from England. From Edith Chadwick to Marvinder.

My Dear Marvi,

Daddy says you're going to be married. I can't believe it! Why, you're the same age as me, and I'm not going to get married for aeons and aeons of time. I consider myself a child! Of course Mummy and Daddy explained it all to me. Mummy says your mother, Jhoti, married at the same time as she did — except your mother was about twelve and mine was twenty-five! But, then, my mother went to university and was a teacher for a bit. I hope I do the same. But I suppose it is different for you, living in a small Indian village.

Daddy told me that your father has arranged it with the man who was a schoolmaster at Daddy's village school in Deri. I'd be scared marrying a schoolmaster! My friends wanted to know all about arranged marriages. They simply don't understand it at all. I tried to tell them that in some ways it's better if your parents choose your husband, because then it's not all your responsibility. Mummy did wonder whether it was what you wanted, but Daddy said we were not to interfere. I think he still feels guilty that he was the cause of your father leaving India just when you all needed him the most. He says you have your own customs which work for you and we have ours.

Dear Marvi! I wish, I wish, I wish I could come to your wedding. I wish we didn't live so many thousands of miles apart. One day, I know I'll come back to India again. By that time, I might be married too – who knows! We might both have children, even!

I wish I knew exactly what date you will marry, then I could think about you. Mummy says your priest will study your holy book and decide from the Scriptures when is the best time. It's all so strange and so different.

I hope your husband is a good, good man and that you will be very, very happy. Daddy is going to find someone who is coming over to India who might be able to take a wedding present for you. I wish it could be me bringing it. I wish I could see you again – and the village and our old bungalow. Is the palace still there? I know it would be sad to see it and remember what happened. They say you should never go back to a place after you've left it. But I think I still want to see it. I sometimes dream about it. There was nowhere else in the world which was such an exciting place to play.

I hope your mother has been able to look after the grave of the twins. Please, Marvi, could you make sure their grave is cared for?

I hope Jaspal is being good and not getting into lots of fights. Give him my love.

Now I really am stopping. I think about you every day. Write soon. Good Luck on the day.

Lots and lots of love,

Your very best friend,

Edith

'You shouldn't be writing to those Britishers,' Jaspal had spat angrily, when he saw the letter come for Marvinder from England. 'You shouldn't have anything more to do with them.'

'Why, Jaspal? Why have you become like this? The Chadwicks were your friends too – the twins and Edith. You liked Edith when we were in England. Why have you changed?'

'Because our friendship with them weakens us. That's what the nihang says and I believe him. They belong to the past. We should forget them. You should forget them. Being friends with them will only harm you. The British were our enemies.'

'But the Chadwicks have never harmed us. How can you say such things? They have always been our friends. If it hadn't been for them, how would we have got home again to find Mother?'

Jaspal yelled angrily. 'The trouble with you is you're too soft. You don't know your friends from your enemies.'

'And do you, dear brother?' cried Marvinder, provoked into anger. 'Do you know the difference? If you are friends with Nazakhat – a Muslim – then why should I not stay friends with the Chadwicks? Or must everyone be our enemies now?'

'Aaaaagh!' Jaspal snarled with disgust and stormed off leaving Marvinder furious and confused. She strode along the shore of the lake towards the palace. The sight of Nazakhat calmly spinning stones across the surface made her boil with resentment.

'Hey, you! Nazakhat!' she yelled. Her voice was sharp with anger.

Nazakhat turned, puzzled.

'Where were you and my brother yesterday? Skiving off as usual I suppose. It doesn't make any difference to you, does it? You're not beholden to anyone. Do you know what kind of trouble Jaspal was in the other night, coming back in the middle of the night like that? My father beat him black and blue. I blame you, you're such a bad influence on him. Just because you haven't got a brain in your head, you don't think it matters if Jaspal is nothing but a goatherd or a layabout like you.'

Nazakhat stood staring at her; dumbstruck; sick with the injustice of what she was saying. 'I wasn't with him that night. I don't know what he was up to.' He shook his head hopelessly as he saw she wasn't listening. Then, just as he turned to go, to get away from her hateful words, she raised her arm to bring up her veil across her face. Her sleeve fell back and he saw the bracelet on her wrist.

'It's you?' he cried incredulously. 'I don't believe it. You?'

Unaware of what he was talking about, Marvinder stumbled off to the palace.

Her legs felt leaden as she climbed the steps. She paused as if the effort had made her dizzy. She went to the balcony's edge and saw Nazakhat still spinning stones at the lakeside. Somehow, the energy had gone out of him and the stones barely bounced before sinking to the bottom. She wanted to call out to him, say she was sorry, but she knew he wouldn't have heard her. With a sigh she took out paper, pen and ink and, kneeling over the page, dipped her pen into the inkpot and wrote:

> *Dear Edith,*
> *I'm utterly miserable. I feel I haven't a friend in the world.*
> *If only you were here to talk to me. I don't want to marry.*

*Why should I? I haven't chosen my husband as you will
and Kathleen will. My father has arranged a marriage with
a man older than himself! Would your father do such a
thing? Even Mr O'Grady wouldn't do such a thing. I
am utterly miserable and sometimes think I'd rather be
dead . . .'*

She set the letter aside. No, she couldn't send that. She tried to
write another, but gave up on that one too.

She got to her feet. She paced the terrace, walking round
all four sides. What was the use of writing? It was too late.
Edith wouldn't get the letter for ages. And when she did, what
difference would it make? The matter had been settled
all along. Her father, Govind, must have written to the
Chadwicks even before Bahadur came formally to talk
about arrangements. She was trapped. She had no power. No
freedom.

And now Jaspal was going away. Suddenly, he had
become a stranger. He had spoken to her as though he had
a cauldron of hatred bubbling inside him. He had been her
closest friend.

She climbed to the highest point. She looked across to the
lake. The shore was empty now. Nazakhat had gone. She
gripped the edge of the balustrade and leaned over till her
feet left the ground. She see-sawed on her stomach, looking
down, down to within one of the curves of the eaves; there, a

huge bees' nest hung – a planet of sweetness all in itself, dangling in space, while around it, the bees swarmed in a cloud, seemingly chaotic, yet each with its own defined task. She watched it for a while, overcome with hopelessness and looked beyond the bees' nest to the flagstones below. How easy it would be – how easy just to let go.

A protective hand began to stretch out behind her, ready to drag her back. It almost touched her when she brought her feet down on to safe ground again. Unseen, the hand withdrew silently. Marvinder pressed her forehead against the balustrade, trying to extract some of its strength for herself. Tears slid hopelessly down her cheeks. After a while her tears dried and she lifted her head. She went back to her writing materials and took out a fresh piece of paper. She dropped to her knees and took up her pen. She dipped it into the inkpot and, instead of writing 'Dear Edith' she wrote:

> *Dear Patrick,*
>
> *I am to be married off. It has all been arranged. The priest has decided it will be after the rains in October. I don't want to marry, but I have no choice. Please don't think badly of me.*
>
> *Whenever I think of truth and beauty, I shall always think of you.*
>
> *I hope you will remember me sometimes.*
>
> *I'm glad you are happy in the navy.*

I hope you will come and visit us if your ship docks in India and you have the time.

Much love,

Marvi

The rains came. Marvinder watched them come, day by day, from the roof of the palace. She saw the great, grey, elephantine clouds first drifting, then stampeding across the heavens and finally bursting, as if God would flood the world and wipe it out all over again.

The long, white road turned into a river of mud.

Marvinder prepared for her wedding day.

14 The first circle

In the first circling, the marriage rite has begun.

Red. The colour swam before his sore eyes; the eyes which were doomed to remain open and never rest behind shuttered lids. The last red these eyes had seen was the blood which had flowed when they massacred his family. Since then, he could hardly bear to look at the colour. Even the red of hibiscus or bougainvillaea or the tulip heads of the scarlet bell tree had made him turn away his gaze, sick to the stomach with remembrance.

He heaved open the lid of the huge, dusty trunk. It creaked on its rusty hinges. He peered into its dark depths; for a moment it was like looking into a pool of blood. Red swam before his eyes. Red pain. He slammed shut the lid and, for some moments, knelt in despair before the trunk gasping out his sorrow. Then, again, he opened the lid. This time he put his hands inside. His fingers were submerged into the red and made contact; not with the sticky red of blood, but the cool, radiant red of silk and muslin – the red of good fortune; the red of the wedding garments – the dupatta, the salwaar kameez. Through the sensitive tips of his fingers, he felt the gold threads woven through like sunbeams; the embroidered patterns coiling round the neck of the tunic and down the sleeves and across the chest. And, when he held up the dupatta, it was as if water trickled through his fingers, so fine it felt, that a bride's cheek would not feel one stitch of roughness as she brought it forward to hide her face.

Piece by piece, he lifted out the marriage clothes and laid them in order on the low divan. Then he found a number of packages, roughly wrapped in old newspaper and tied with string. One by one, he opened them up. Red. Red. Always red. The red of rubies glowed like burning coals. There were rubies edged with pearls, embedded in emeralds and encased in gold. Jewels for the hair, the neck, the ears, the nose, the breast, for the arms and wrists, the ankles and toes. Jewels fit for a princess. A bride's jewels.

Then, all around the room, on chairs and cushions and low tables, he laid out more clothes; more salwaar kameez and dupattas, exquisite sarees and wonderful pieces of cloth:

Benares silk, embroidered shawls of finest Kashmiri wool, thinnest Lucknow cotton, South Indian prints, mirror-stitched blouses from Rajasthan, and more precious metals and jewels: gold and silver and gems gleaming from brooches and pins and bracelets and bangles and rings and studs. Soon the whole of this low, dark, underground chamber was ablaze with the treasure of a bride's dowry. All that was needed was the bride.

He spoke to her through the wall, his soft voice throbbing like honey bees.

> 'Can I describe the ruin of the palace of my heart?
> Its towers crumbled into dust, its walls are torn apart.'

'Come and let me see you as a bride,' the voice begged her. 'My eyes have known nothing but tears and sorrows for so long. Put on the earrings which came from me and then let me guide you to where the rest of your bride's things are laid out. Be a bride for me – just for one day.'

'But what if . . . ?' whispered Marvinder. Her voice faltered. He heard the edge of fear in her breath; her inner voice of reason telling her to flee.

'I would never harm you. I would as soon dash my body from the highest terrace, than see one hair of your head come to any harm. Believe me.'

'I don't even know your name,' she said.

'Call me Beast.'

Marvinder laughed but wanted to cry.

'Don't laugh,' he said. The voice was serious and demanded attention.

'How can I call you Beast – why, that's no name – and why should you want me to call you such a rude name?'

'Because I am a beast.'

He began to sing. His voice quivering up scales, twining in and out of half-tones and quarter-tones, trembling like water at the rim, then plunging down, refracting through light. It enticed her, mesmerised her, reassured her, drew her into the palace apartments, and she allowed herself to be guided through doors she did not know existed, into rooms she did not know were there. It led her downwards and downwards. A burning lamp was left for her. It lit her way along narrow passages smelling of earth and water, into rooms without windows, where daylight never entered. Then she stopped. She stood before a door. It was a heavy wooden door. His voice called to her from behind it.

She pushed it open. It was like entering the heart of the sun. There were saucers of oil with flaming wicks, all blazing with light that dazzled her eyes. On a divan lay the bridal clothes and the wedding trousseau.

'Put them on,' said the voice. 'Put them on as if this were your wedding day. Put on all the jewellery – all of it – even rings on the toes.'

'Why?' she asked, bewildered. 'And why can't I see you?'

'Don't ask, my dear, don't ask,' he pleaded. 'You would hate me. I am a beast. I was turned into a beast by war and hatred. My face and body are too dreadful to look upon – but worse still are my deeds. I have behaved like a wild animal. I have murdered and tortured; I have rampaged and torched people's homes; I have destroyed people's lives. I have orphaned little children. What was done to you was done by people like me. Then I became a victim. Whatever terrors and tortures I did to others were in turn done to me. I was a victim as well as a killer. I saw my home destroyed, my children slain – my daughter . . .' His voice broke, and for a while he was silent as he struggled with his emotions. 'This was her dowry,' he finally whispered. 'I think I am doomed to everlasting damnation. I came back to my district and the tomb of the saint to try and earn forgiveness. I cry to Allah – but hear nothing in return. Then you came. Full of truth and beauty. And I began to believe again.'

'So it is you drumming at the tomb each night,' she said.

'Yes. I drum to keep away evil spirits, though I myself am evil.'

For a moment there was silence. She looked around and beyond the circle of flames into the impenetrable darkness. His voice was everywhere. She wondered if he was looking at her now. She bowed her head. 'What must I do?'

'Put on the bridal clothes. Be a bride for me – just for a

while. Be my daughter. I will not touch you. I just want to look at you in all the finery – and remember life was good once, and could be good again. I leave you now. And when you are dressed, come back up to the highest terrace.'

'Will I find my way?'

'Oh, yes. I will leave a light at every corner.'

It took a long time. Putting on all the clothes and the jewellery; a princess would have had several handmaidens to help her, especially when the loose hair had to be re-plaited and threaded with pearls.

But at last she stood there shimmering and looked about her. Then she saw someone. There, just out of the halo of flames, a person stared at her: a young woman, unrecognisable; a princess – perhaps – yes – the ghost of a princess who had once lived in this palace; so beautiful, so bejewelled; so graceful. Marvinder backed away, her hand stuffed in her mouth, her legs weakening till she nearly fell. The image retreated. She stopped, took a step or two forward and then realised. It was herself. She stood before a long mirror and her own mirror image gazed back at her there in the darkness.

When she stepped out on to the roof, the daylight was astounding. The vivid blue of the sky and the green of the trees made her feel as if she had just come back to life. She pulled the veil right down over her face – partly because that was customary for a bride, but also because the glare was more then her eyes could bear, and she looked at the world through the red haze of her dupatta.

'Walk.' His voice startled her. It was so close. She felt she could almost feel his breath on her neck.

'This is your kingdom now – as far as the eye can see is yours. It was once mine, but I give it all to you. Walk like a sovereign queen; claim it with your eye.' She walked and she did feel like a queen as the soft garments flowed around her. When she had circled the whole terrace, and was back where she started, he said, 'Lift your veil so that I may see your face once more.'

'Only if you will let me see your face.' Suddenly, she felt emboldened. He owed it to her. She had to see him. 'I want to see you. I've seen ugliness and death. You couldn't upset me. No one with a voice so beautiful could be as ugly as that.'

'No, no, no!' he groaned in anguish. 'You don't know. Don't ask to see me. You will hate me.'

'How could I hate you? You are good. I know you are. Whatever you say you have done, you are good, so your face too will be good. It will be beautiful. I wouldn't be afraid.'

'Let me sing to you instead. Let my voice be my face.'

He began to sing.

But Marvinder was determined to find him, so as he sang, instead of giving in to the hypnotic waves of sound which before had drugged her, she began to calculate where he could be hiding. There must be secret passages in these walls, with spyholes. She knew that many palaces and forts were built in this way, with secret underground tunnels and chambers within chambers as a protection should they be overrun by enemies. She leaned against the walls, pressing her hands and her ears to the cool stone. Gradually, she closed in on the source of the voice. She pulled the veil tighter over her face so that he shouldn't be able to follow her eyes as they searched for a give-away gap in the stone through which he was watching her.

Normally she would have missed the thin pool of dust lying in one spot. But it was exactly the sign she was looking for. Her eye examined the wall and the stone and she saw the slight difference in the layout of the brick. As the song carried on, she edged her way towards it.

Too late, the singer stopped singing. With a quick run, Marvinder dashed over to the spot and, with both hands, pushed hard. The wall became a door and opened.

'Show yourself to me! Show me – dear Beast!' she shouted. But as the words left her lips they were already dying in horror. There before her was the most hideous creature she had ever seen or imagined in her most dreadful nightmares. She opened her mouth trying to find enough air to scream, but fainted before a sound left her throat.

15 The second circle

In the second circling, divine music is heard.

The drumming at the Muslim tomb continued. Even the monsoon rain, roaring down loud as a waterfall, or the nights when there were thunderstorms with hailstones as large as goose eggs, and lightning lacerated the sky, didn't halt the ceaseless drumming. Then, just as the rains began to die away and the monsoon clouds rolled on eastwards, Marvinder disappeared.

She had not been seen since she took her father's midday meal to him in the fields. By evening, Jhoti was anxiously scouring the district asking everyone, 'Have you seen Marvinder?' With nightfall, her family were frantic. Mother, father, brother, her future husband and half the village, combed every place they could think of, starting with the palace, but they found nothing – not one clue as to where she had gone. It was as if the earth had opened up and swallowed her.

Nazakhat lay restlessly on his string bed wondering about Marvinder. There was a sense of disturbance everywhere, as if her disappearance had resonated far beyond those who loved her. A wind banged a piece of loose corrugated iron on a roof, dogs barked incessantly and, from some dwelling in the village, a baby cried and cried inconsolably. He knew Jaspal would be out there somewhere, searching for his sister. He had been distraught when she vanished. After all, he had failed to protect her.

Where was she? Nazakhat tried to imagine. Was she lying helplessly somewhere, calling for help? Or had she run away to escape marriage to a man older than her father? And if so, where had she gone? Was she alive or dead?

All the while, as a background to his thoughts, the drumming beat at the Muslim tomb. It was low and constant and relentless. It was eerie. Sometimes gangs of lads went along there, determined to silence the drumming and chase away the drummer. But once their feet stood on the ancient flagstones, their loud rude voices faltered and their boastful courage drained away. The great dome towered over them, stark, stripped, martyred; and the youths felt their presence was sacrilegious. After a few rowdy jokes, they trickled away into the undergrowth, retrieving their dignity by muttering about unquiet spirits and inventing stories about ghosts and ghouls. And the drumming continued.

Only Nazakhat felt he had the right to go to the tomb. He had been determined to find out who was the drummer and was only waiting for the right time. He had prepared himself as if he were going on an expedition: he acquired a torch, some rope and matches, a bottle to contain water and a cloth bag in which he would store nuts and bananas.

But when the moment came, Nazakhat was unprepared. That night, sleepless with wondering about Marvinder, he saw Jungli creeping out of the room. Nazakhat cursed the child and stumbled out after him. In the dark grey lanes, even the dogs weren't awake. He could hear the drum beat. It had diminished now to a regular struck beat, like the pulse of someone who slept.

He glimpsed Jungli, bounding on all fours. Jungli saw Nazakhat and leaped over to him – circling him, nudging his knees – then bounded away.

'Come back, you big nuisance,' grumbled Nazakhat, trying to grab him. 'We don't want to lose you too.'

Jungli barked in the darkness like a fox and streaked away along his own tracks and trails, following smells and signs known only to him; sometimes rushing ahead and disappearing, then retracing his steps, sniffing and snorting as if he identified clues and signs.

Nazakhat struggled to keep up. He couldn't go back to bed till he had recaptured the wild child. Every now and then Jungli would rush up to Nazakhat and lick his fingers and Nazakhat would try and grab him, but somehow, Jungli had a peculiar strength and was as wriggly as a fish, and he would slip through Nazakhat's grasping fingers and bound away out of sight again.

And all the time, the drum was beating, boom, boom, boom.

Suddenly, it stopped. Nazakhat stopped. The night sky was getting lighter, with streaks of pink. He looked around him and gave a deep breath. His hunt for Jungli had brought him very close to the tomb. Then he knew it. Now was the moment he must look for the drummer. He wondered whether to rush back and collect the kit he had so carefully put together. But somehow, he felt he would lose the moment if he turned away.

Nazakhat reached the walls of the tomb. The silence was eerie now that the drumming had ceased. 'Heh! Jungli! Come on! Let's go!' he called softly. He kicked off his sandals and clambered up on to the plinth. The monsoon had brought out snakes and spiders and all sorts of scuttling, scurrying and stinging creatures. He wished he had his torch. Creatures slithered over his foot or skimmed across his face.

A flickering light coming from below threw a very soft orange glow as far as the bottom step. Nazakhat could hardly breathe with excitement. Was the drummer still there? He crept down the steps. At the bottom, keeping his back pressed to the wall, he peered round into the chamber. A clay shallow dish with oil and wick was burning on a ledge.

The tomb dominated the small lower chamber, like a low hillock of marble. He took the oil lamp and held up its flickering light. Nazakhat moved round the walls, examining every part, wondering if there was another exit.

'So it is you!'

A torch switched on and Nazakhat found himself targeted in a pool of blinding light.

'You pig of a dog. Insulting the people who have protected you!'

'Jaspal! Is that you?' Nazakhat tried to duck out of the light and see the voice.

'I knew it must be you — you, a Muslim.'

'For pity's sake. You are mistaken. It is not me. Look! Can you see a drum? I came to get Jungli back. He ran out in the night. I'm his keeper — remember? I followed him here. For God's sake, Jaspal, get that light out of my eyes.'

Jaspal lowered the beam and emerged out of the shadows holding his torch like a weapon. Nazakhat couldn't see his face, but felt an anger as lethal as a poisonous snake.

'There is something going on. I know that — but it isn't to do with me, I tell you!' Nazakhat cried desperately. 'Marvinder is missing; Jungli keeps coming here and none of us knows who is drumming night after night. Don't you realise? The man must have been here – just a few minutes ago. Look – I found this oil lamp. I was about to look for . . .'

'Look for what? I'm not interested in your drummer. Where's my sister? That's all I want to know.' Jaspal's voice broke with fear. 'Where could she have gone? I've searched the palace, but nothing. Not one clue. Oh God!' His hand holding the torch dropped to his side and the torchlight fell in a small pool on the floor. Nazakhat lifted the oil lamp – so pale in comparison.

'Bhai!' Nazakhat said gently, reaching out to touch his best friend's arm. 'Let me help you look for her?'

'What's it to you? You sort out your own problems. I'm going to carry on looking for my sister.' Jaspal rushed out of the tomb, leaving his friend in the dim light of the oil lamp.

Nazakhat would have followed, but something about the wall caught his eye – even in that dim light. He looked at the letters of the Koran. They were formed by inlay of shining jet, which hadn't been pillaged. The swirls and curves of the Arabic script rose upwards and round in the outline of an arch. He ran a hand over the letters, feeling their raised shapes beneath his fingers. All the time, he was pushing his weight against the marble walls.

He was standing in the very centre of the arch like someone on the threshold of a doorway when he felt the wall move.

'Hey, Jaspal, bhai! Oh my god!'

He rushed out of the tomb, hissing into the darkness. 'Jaspal! Look! The wall! It moved. Jaspal, come back!' But there was no reply. Jaspal had gone.

Nazakhat returned excitedly. He pressed his hands all over the wall with flat palms. He whispered with intense excitement. 'Yes, yes, yes.' He pressed again; harder. The wall swung open to reveal a long, low tunnel disappearing into pitch darkness.

The boy stared with astonishment. He stepped over the threshold into the deathlike darkness. Then he shuddered and staggered back to the steps. He climbed up into the dawn light, gulping the fresh air. He tried to fight the fears which suddenly overwhelmed him. What if the door slammed shut and he was locked in the tomb for ever, buried alive? His courage slipped away.

A soft wet tongue licked his fingers and two arms flung themselves round his knees. Nazakhat laughed with relief. 'Oh! It's you!' He hugged the funny, bony, little body of the wild child. 'Heh! Jaspal!' he called out. 'Jungli's here! The little devil! I thought I'd find you here.'

Jungli wriggled free and bounded away down the steps into the tomb. With a surge, Nazakhat's courage returned. If Jungli came to no harm, then why should he be afraid? He went back down.

As he went back through the arch, Nazakhat forced himself to think rationally. This was no ghost or spirit who came to drum at the tomb. This was a human being – like himself – and brave too. Well, he would be brave and he would think for himself. Think how to go about this search. Nazakhat looked round for a large stone and carried it down into the flickering light of the tomb. The door had swung to a close. Nazakhat pushed the wall again, and again the door swung open. He heaved the stone into the hinge and propped the door ajar. There was no sign of Jungli. Nazakhat whistled for him, but when he didn't reappear, decided to proceed.

The tunnel ahead was pitch black. Nazakhat took the oil lamp. It was awkward, as he had to crouch and sometimes crawl along the tunnel. On and on he went, trying not to imagine what fate could befall him if he got trapped down here and praying that the oil would last out.

The tunnel suddenly descended steeply, and there was a powerful smell of mud and weeds and water. When it straightened out, he came to a fork in the tunnel. He didn't know which path to follow. Where was Jungli? He called his name softly and whistled and wished he would come. He was sure Jungli would know which one to take. He stared at the choice, then shrugged and arbitrarily chose the left fork. After a while it began to rise. A waft of fresh air made him breathe deeply. He quickened his pace at the thought of getting above ground again. The ascent of stone steps was completely un-expected and he nearly stumbled over them. From his knees he stared up to a square of blue sky. With open mouth, gulping in the air, he scrambled hands and feet like an animal above ground.

'Oh! If only Jaspal could see this!' Nazakhat couldn't believe where he found himself. He was standing in the cupola, on the fishing island, right in the very centre of the lake.

'Oh my! Jaspal! You should see this! Look what I've found! Oh my!' Nazakhat was overwhelmed with his discovery. All these years – and he had never heard even a rumour about secret tunnels from the tomb under the lake to the island. But, once his excitement died down, he began to think again about the drummer. Is this where the drummer came from? There was no sign of anyone having been here, camped here, eaten food. No drum. He glanced around him – looking at the shore and the palace, floating like a boat among the tops of the trees.

But the sun was quite high now and ascending with every second. Sunlight enfolded the old building in a blaze of gold which made his eyes narrow with the brightness.

Then he heard the singing. Low, high – a man's voice or perhaps a woman's – it had such range, he couldn't be sure. It came from below the surface of the lake, scuttering with the ripples; it came from the stones on which he stood, reverberating up through the soles of his feet. It surrounded him. When at last Nazakhat could bring himself to move, he took up the oil lamp and descended the steps. The singing was louder. He moved back down the tunnel, crouching and cowering as the tunnel roof lowered over his head. He reached the fork. The singing was coming from the left – he was sure of it – and turned to the left. The tunnel seemed to go on for ever. Here there was no smell of fresh air or daylight, just the stifling stench of rotting weeds and undergrowth and earth. This is what it must smell like if you are buried alive. His panic rose in his stomach and up his throat.

Suddenly, he saw a door ahead of him. A large wooden door. With a cry, he flung himself on to it. The door swung open and he found himself blinded by a blaze of flickering lights from dozens of oil lamps.

The singing was here. Yet he couldn't see anyone. It came from this very room, he was sure, reverberating all around him. It was loud, it was passionate, it was spectacular in its brilliance. The voice rose up the scale, higher and higher – and when it reached the top it went on rising.

'Where are you? Where, where, where?' Nazakhat stumbled round the room searching for the singer.

The singing gave way to a high-pitched wail, which turned into a shriek, then a howling like some demented demon.

Nazakhat fell to his knees and crouched on the floor with his head between his arms. He was weeping with terror; weeping at his own cowardice, certain in that moment that he was going to die. The shrieking and wailing went on and on and on. Shrieks that reminded him of the massacre of his family.

He was barely aware of a slight movement from behind. Jungli streaked past him and disappeared into the blaze of light. Slowly, Nazakhat raised his head and gradually made out a divan with a figure all in scarlet lying on it. The wild child flung himself on to the figure, gurgling and laughing. Then he leaped down and rushed to Nazakhat. He grabbed his hand and tugged him towards the divan.

The figure was awakening. It was a woman, dressed in scarlet, her face completely covered by her dupatta. She raised herself on one elbow, her head hanging as if she were still asleep. The howling voice turned to singing again. The harsh screams softened to notes and phrases, smoothed away, undulating sweetly, soft as a lullaby.

He thought he was looking at a phantom, until she brushed aside the veil which covered her face.

'Marvinder!'

Jungli stood on two feet in the middle of the room, swaying in ecstasy and the beast sang divine music.

16 The third circle

In the third circling, the love of God has been awakened in the heart.

It is said to be the law of Brahma, when a man dresses his daughter and adorns her and he himself gives her as a gift to a man he has summoned.

We dare not ask what happened to Marvinder, my daughter, during the time she was missing. Nazakhat found her at the tomb, dressed like a bride, as if she had gone through some dreadful marriage ceremony with a husband from the dead. What kind of selfish father am I, that all I dreaded was that it would mean Bahadur Singh would now reject her and that I would have to keep my daughter for ever?

* * *

Nazakhat told Jaspal he had found Marvinder. He led Jaspal to the tomb, then rushed off to inform Govind. Govind came with a bullock cart and they wrapped Marvinder up in a white sheet to hide the shame of the strange marriage scarlet of her clothes. They surrounded her with bundles of straw and cane stalks to shield her from inquisitive eyes, and smuggled her home.

'Strip her of every stick of these clothes and burn them,' ordered Govind harshly. 'And here, you should take these, since it is you who found her,' and Govind roughly tore off all the jewels which had adorned his daughter and threw them at Nazakhat.

Before he summoned Bahadur, he interrogated Marvinder. 'Where have you been? Who gave you these clothes and these jewels? What have you been up to – dishonouring our family and our name? Don't you realise what you have done?' In his fury, he raised his hand many times to strike Marvinder when she seemed unwilling or unable to explain how she came to be in this state. He wanted to beat the truth out of her but something just held him back; some voice at the back of his head which seemed to warn him not to lay a finger on her.

She didn't seem distressed by her experience. Indeed, she looked almost serene and, finally, Govind stopped trying to force out any more information. He ordered Jhoti to take Marvinder to the river and scrub her clean, while he lit a fire to burn the bridal garments which he had not provided. Bitterly, he dropped the items one by one into the flames and watched them shrivel into blackened ashes. They seemed to accuse him. Had there once been another father who loved his daughter so much he had managed to provide her with clothes fit for a princess? If only he could have passed Marvinder through the flames and annihilated his conscience and her dishonour.

Finally, when he had composed himself, Govind sent Nazakhat to fetch Bahadur and tell him Marvinder was found. Govind hardly dared believe that Bahadur would now wish to proceed with the marriage.

There was a last flurry of monsoon rain as Nazakhat stood on the schoolmaster's verandah to tell him the news. A moist wind rushed through the leaves of the trees and shook blossoms scattering across the yard. Bahadur listened quietly and calmly. There was more to the story, Bahadur was sure of it, but Nazakhat would only say that he had found Marvinder at the Muslim saint's tomb dressed in bride's clothes and that no one knew how she came to be there.

'Don't tell anyone about the singer, Nazakhat,' Marvinder had beseeched him as he dragged her away from that dreadful room of fire. 'Don't tell anyone – not even Jaspal. Don't destroy the guardian of the tomb. He was guarding your saint. If they find him, they will kill him. Do you promise me?'

Nazakhat had not promised anything till they burst out of

the ground into the fresh air – not knowing what time of day it was or what passage of time had elapsed since he entered the tomb.

'How can you not tell? Look at you!' Nazakhat had exclaimed. 'Was it the drummer who gave you these clothes and jewels? Who is he? Have you seen him?'

'Have you seen him?' The question had nearly made her faint again with the memory. Him? A man? No, not a man – not a human of this world. A beast. Yet she wouldn't give him away.

'I have seen no man,' Marvinder had answered.

When Bahadur arrived at Marvinder's home, she was dressed in a pale blue salwaar kameez. Her face was completely covered by her dupatta and she stood with bowed head next to her father. Jhoti, after humbly greeting the schoolmaster, shrank away to the kitchen to make tea. Jaspal refused to be present.

Govind began a long explanation, certain that he must do everything in his power to make the incident seem trivial so that Bahadur wouldn't reject Marvinder. But Bahadur interrupted him politely. 'I would like to speak alone to your daughter,' he said. 'Would you consent to her taking a walk with me? You or your wife may follow behind.'

Govind shrugged. 'If you think there is anything to be gained from talking to her. I haven't managed to get anything out of her.'

They walked down to the shore of the lake. Jhoti trailed them at a distance. Marvinder would have walked seven steps behind, as is the custom, but Bahadur insisted she walk level with him. 'I don't want to speak to you over my shoulder,' he said.

So Marvinder walked in parallel but at arm's length apart, while Bahadur began to talk to her.

'Do you object to marrying me?' he asked.

Marvinder was surprised at his question. She had expected to be asked about her disappearance.

'No, no!' she protested, though her voice trailed away with the lie. 'It's . . . it's not you. It's just that I don't want to marry,' she stammered out loud, though inside her head she could hear Patrick's puzzled voice saying, 'You couldn't marry a man you didn't love, could you, Marvi?'

'I would like to study – though I don't know how. We have no money,' Marvinder tried to explain. 'I liked school when I was in England, but I was so far behind. I would like to go to a place of learning where I can learn more and where I could play my violin even.'

'I am a teacher. Be my pupil,' said Bahadur. 'I can teach you about literature and philosophy. I can help you to read more advanced books. As for your violin playing, I believe there is a British lady, a missionary who stayed behind. She lives in Amritsar. She used to teach music at the girls' school. Perhaps she would teach you.'

Marvinder looked Bahadur straight in the face for the very first time – in the Western way. It was a kind face. She knew he was kind, and his light brown eyes looked directly into hers as an equal. She lowered her eyes again and drew her veil across her face as if to compensate for her boldness. 'How can I do all these things and still be married?' she asked.

'You can, if that's what we both agree. Don't you see? I want what you want. I too want you to have more learning. Then you can help me better. I support your desire to advance yourself.' Then Bahadur talked and talked. He told her about all his ambitions for re-building his school – even going further and turning it into a college to train teachers – men and young women like her. 'Years ago, I listened to Gandhiji. I went to his ashram and sat at his feet. I wanted to be a teacher like him. You could be a teacher too. We will not be an ordinary couple, you and I.' Bahadur stopped walking and turned to face her so that he could impart to her the force of his feelings. He was aware that she listened intently. So he continued. 'We would look beyond what we want for our-selves; beyond family and money. We would have a mission to serve our new country. It's what Gandhiji would have wanted. He wanted young women like you to have justice and fair treatment. That is what I want. Now that he is dead, it is up to us to bring his dreams alive. Not because they were useless dreams, but because they were right. Right for India. That is what I believe. But I can't do it alone. You are young, I know

– and it probably disgusts you to consider marrying a man like me – even older than your father. But India needs us both; your youth, because independent India is young, and my age, because India is ancient. Help me, Marvinder. If you truly do not wish to marry me, then I will tell your father that we shall not proceed. But I think we could serve each other well. Be my wife and help me.'

Marvinder stared out over the steely waters of the lake. A grey crane flew slow and low across the surface, its neck and feet outstretched, its wide wings flapping lazily but deep, with just enough force to keep its body in flight.

'Do you want to know what happened to me?' she asked.

'I only want to know what you wish to tell me,' said Bahadur.

'I didn't want to disappear. I didn't run away to escape you. I don't really know what happened, except I did not dishonour you or my family.'

'Then let's say no more on the matter,' he said.

Bahadur stopped and they both watched the crane fly over the lake, then land at a distance and merge into the tall reeds. Without exchanging any further words, they turned round and went back to Marvinder's home. He thought they would part without her saying another word. He thought perhaps everything he had told her – right from his heart – had fallen on stony ground, but just before she climbed her verandah steps, she turned round and half drew the veil away from her face. 'Sir!' she said quietly. 'Thank you. Tell my father that the marriage will proceed. I will try to be a suitable wife for you.'

'I can ask no more,' replied Bahadur. With a respectful short bow, he took his bicycle, kicked back the stand and cycled away.

17 The fourth circle

In the fourth circling we have found the Eternal Lord.

The sun had already set by the time the bus paused briefly at the roadside, and a young white man got off with a naval canvas holdall. Although the bus had been crowded to bursting point, still, they had managed to make room for the traveller, creating a respectful space around him.

He knew only one word: 'Deri'. He said it often as the bus stopped from time to time, and other passengers nodded their heads reassuringly. They would see him right, their eager, friendly glances told him. He had expected hostility. How swiftly people forgot past humiliations, he thought.

He supposed it was foolish to have set off into the

countryside, with night so close to falling, but he was unwilling to lose even a single precious hour, in his desire to reach the village.

They pointed him in the direction of a track which left the white road. The traveller took it, though it immediately plunged him into a darkness of thicket and thorn and dusty oblivion.

He fumbled in his holdall for a torch, and flashed its broad beam around him. It caught the yellow eyes of an animal. Startled, it stared at him briefly, before it retreated without even the faintest rustle into the undergrowth.

The track wound ahead of him. Its deep, bullock-cart ruts and evident wear reassured him and he strode along it with more confidence, his torchlight glancing from side to side. He was brought to a standstill when the path forked decisively. Which way? Both paths looked equally sure of themselves. Both led somewhere – but which one would take him to the village? He flashed his torch around; walked along one a little way but seemed to plunge deeper and deeper into fields, so he backtracked and set off along the other prong. A great shining rose to meet him like a dark mirror, reflecting pale stars and the faintest outline of a new moon. The path gave way to a shore and he realised he had reached an expanse of water.

He had been prepared to unroll a sleeping-bag from his holdall and spend the night by the shore – it felt safer – better than in the thicket where there might be snakes. Then, across the dark water, the outline of a small, domed roof seemed to float like a lotus and he saw a light, glimmering, pale, bobbing – fragile as a firefly. Was he mistaken? Was it a star reflecting in the water? But no, it moved. The traveller stared at it as it traversed steadily towards the shore.

Someone rowed across the lake. A night fisherman? The light reached the shore and began to move inland. The traveller hauled together his belongings and began to run, not wanting to lose the light and his possible guide to the village. From time to time he lost sight of it, as he plunged into deep undergrowth, but then it would reappear just ahead of him, drawing him on. But finally it was gone.

The traveller stopped, his eyes adjusting to a vast dark shape which rose before him, and he realised he stood before an enormous building. He flashed his torch before him. He could see ornate arches and pillars and steps leading up to a broad verandah – but all crumbling and damaged and peeling with neglect. He moved round the outer walls, peering through the windows, but there was no glimmer of light to indicate any human presence.

'Well, better still, to park myself here for the night; more protection than out in the open,' the traveller muttered out loud. He crossed the verandah, entered through a doorway and into an inner courtyard. It would feel safer to have something firm against his back, and unrolling his sleeping-bag, he tucked himself into the wall of the courtyard and quickly fell into an exhausted sleep.

He wasn't aware of the eyes without lids which spied on him in the darkness, or the scarred, bare feet which stood by his head. All night long, the watcher paced, silent as a panther, occasionally pausing to study the sleeping figure by the light of a dim lamp. How can the clamour of emotion be so soundless? How could the fierce hatred and jealousy for the sleeper not reverberate around the walls, or echo a deep despairing wail among the pillars? For the watcher knew who this man was.

People wondered why the drummer at the tomb was silent that night.

Dawn was a fierce awakening. The screeching of crows and the loud slapping of pigeons brought the traveller to his senses, out of the troublesome dreams which had tossed him through the night. A grey light illuminated the building into which he had crawled, and he gazed at it with wonder – at the pillars and patterned tiles and the terraces rising up and up, and the crumbling grandeur of ornate balustrades and balconies. The patch of silver dawn sky hung above him with high-flying kites wheeling slowly in and out of his vision.

Full of curiosity, he began exploring and soon found himself climbing the stone steps to the upper terraces and the roof. He would surely be able to find his bearings from there – perhaps even see the little village which was the target of his journey. On one side, he saw as far as the Himalayas, on another, the lake he had walked along last night; but to the west, a white early morning mist hung over the land and the tops of trees seemed to float in a sea of milk, mingling with steam snorted from the nostrils of awakening bullocks and water buffalo. He could identify small brick houses and low mud-built dwellings clustered round two or three mango trees. Already a man stood at the edge of a village pond, bathing and praying, and beneath the one vast neem tree, a child chewed on a twig. The traveller knew he had arrived.

Energised and excited, he sprang, two at a time, down the steps and rapidly bundled up his sleeping-bag. He would make for the shore to wash and shave before proceeding further. Briefly, he paused on the terrace feeling like a rajah. Looking around him, he made out ancient walkways along which had once been carefully nurtured flowerbeds. Among the wild shrubbery and undergrowth, he could see cultivated roses now rambling free – wild as weeds – red and white and orange and pink. He leaped down into the wilderness garden, smiling at the thought of what a perfect offering they would make.

He plucked one, two three – marvelling at their half-closed heads, still wet with dew.

Suddenly, a dreadful cry froze the blood in his veins and the roses fell scattering from his hand.

'How dare you! How dare you!'

The traveller turned in terror to see where this monstrous voice came from. A voice so savage it could have come from the throat of a beast.

'How dare you enter my garden and pluck my roses.'

The traveller didn't understand the words and didn't wait for a translation. 'Leave this place. Leave this place, I tell you. You should not have come.' The words echoed incomprehensibly in his ears as he fled from the garden. 'You should not have come!'

The traveller fled, stumbling through the undergrowth like a hunted animal, ducking and diving in and out of bushes and trees as if demons pursued him. He burst through some long grass to find himself at the edge of the lake – and there just beyond was the start of a few small huts.

He moved nearer to habitation, glancing all round him to be certain he had not been followed. Finally, reassured and somewhat shamefaced at his panic, he stripped off his clothes and waded into the lake, splashing himself and completely immersing his body to wash away his dread.

Every now and then he looked around him and glimpsed parts of the upper terraces of the building where he had spent the night. He felt glad to be alive. He wondered who lived there in a place so wild and neglected and yet who was so resentful of any one trespassing into the tangled grounds to pick a few wild roses.

Suddenly, the traveller shuddered with unease. The garden and the roses and the dreadful ranting seemed like a bad omen. Why had he made all that effort? Spent precious leave journeying all the way to India on a boat and trains and buses – for what? He wasn't interested in seeing Govind – he despised the man. He didn't know Jhoti. Jaspal had been a pest – they had all been glad when he'd gone. But Marvinder. He had left her as a girl in England, but in his mind, she had grown and grown; now she was a woman ready for marriage, and suddenly he had been struck with a great urgency to see her and had written to her immediately. He wanted to see whether his feelings for her were just a romantic fantasy or real. Of all the people he had met in his life, he suddenly felt with almost unbearable intensity that she was the most important. She had spoken to him of truth and beauty – and only now, did it all come clear and he understood.

A rattle of drums started up and a high-pitched tune pierced the air. A cluster of children hurtled across the fields, yelling with excitement. It lifted his spirits too and he hurried out of the water and towelled himself dry. He pulled on a pair of cotton trousers and a white shirt and combed his hair, then, tossing his holdall over a shoulder, he headed in the direction of the music.

A young boy herding goats pointed out the house – a simple red brick house with a front verandah. He was told that was where Govind lived with his wife, Jhoti, and their two children, Marvinder and Jaspal.

The traveller paused in the shade of the neem tree, camouflaged by the dappled shade. He was struck by a sense of triumph, almost a feeling of power. He had formulated a plan and a timetable which had involved crossing thousands

145

of miles. He had now reached a small house in a tiny village in the middle of a vast continent and in that house was the person he had set out to find.

Festive drummers were thundering out their rhythms, their sound filling the neighbourhood; temple bells ching-chinged like dancing feet, and the Indian oboes blew so high-pitched, it was as if they were determined that their sounds should reach the gods themselves in their heavens. People were converging from everywhere. There was an air of gaiety and bustle, laughter and chattering. They had put on their best clothes and the women had adorned themselves in heavy jewellery. Girls carried flowers and garlands and handfuls of offerings, and all the time the music got louder and more shrill. The musicians came into sight with an entourage of riotous children, some of them clutching tin cans, which they beat in place of a drum, and headed for a large billowing canopy erected on spindly bamboo legs, which swayed and wobbled. There they settled themselves down cross-legged, prepared to play on for the next sixteen hours.

The traveller was aware of a slight movement at his side and turned to find an old man resting his chin on a long, gnarled stick.

'Are you knowing this area, sahib?' the old man asked politely in English.

'No. No. This is my first visit to India,' replied the traveller.

'Oh-ho!' The old man sighed, as though he envied anyone

coming to India for the first time and discovering all the wonderful places and treasures. 'Have you seen the Golden Temple, the Taj Mahal and the Red Fort in Delhi? Have you been to Benares and Jaipur and seen the wondrous temples and palaces?'

'No, no, I haven't yet. I came straight here,' said the traveller.

'What, may I ask, is so important about this humble village, that you should be coming here before seeing even the Golden Temple?'

'I . . . er . . . I used to know some people – Govind Singh and his children, Jaspal and Marvinder. They lived with us in England.'

'Aye-yi-yi!' The old man clasped his hands together. 'How honoured and grateful the family will be to know that an esteemed Englishman is coming all the way from England to see them. But you are not Mr Chadwick?'

'No, I am not Mr Chadwick. In actual fact, I'm Irish,' said the traveller. 'But yes, I am serving with the British Royal Navy there – National Service. I came all the way from Singapore. Er . . . can you tell me what's going on? All this music and stuff. Is it a festival?'

'You mean you are not knowing? Have you not come specially for the daughter's wedding?'

'Daughter? Which daughter?' the traveller asked alarmed.

'Why, Govind Singh has only one daughter, sahib. Marvinder. She is marrying Bahadur Singh, the local schoolmaster.'

Now the traveller knew why he had come all this way. A pain seared through his stomach and the involuntary gasp he gave startled the old man.

'Are you ill, sahib?'

The traveller dropped his bag to the ground and collapsed on to it in despair. 'So soon?' His shoulders drooped and, suddenly, he looked exhausted.

'I am not understanding you? Are you ill?' repeated the old man.

'No, no! Just tired. Is the family at home? I don't see anyone.' But even as he spoke a woman emerged from the house and stood on the verandah staring hard at him. 'Who's that?' he asked in a sharp whisper.

'Jhoti Kaur, sahib. That is the mother of the bride. She is looking at you, sahib, as though she knows you.'

Jhoti came towards them, pulling her veil across her face. The traveller leaped to his feet holding out a hand. She took it limply, then clasped her hands together and made a namaste. Awkwardly, he did the same.

'Are you Patrick?' she asked in careful English.

'Yes. I am. Did Marvinder tell you?'

'No. She told me nothing. All I knew was that you wrote to her and that I saw . . .'

'Ma'am?' he asked puzzled. 'What did you see? I don't follow.'

'It doesn't matter,' she said sadly, and he wasn't sure if she also added, almost inaudibly, 'but I wish you hadn't come.'

Beyond her, the bamboo curtain shielding the door was held aside and he caught a glimpse of a young woman in red, her shining black hair half plaited, her slim brown hand raised as if reaching out and an expression on her face . . . which told him all he needed to know.

Manu's Law states:

> *In the fire set at the time of marriage, the householder should perform the domestic rituals and the five sacrifices in accordance with the rules, and do his everyday cooking. A householder has five slaughter houses, whose use fetters him: the fireplace, the grindstone, the broom, the mortar and pestle, and the water jar. The great sages devised the five great sacrifices for the householder to do every day to redeem him from all of these slaughter houses successively. The study of the Vedas is the sacrifice to ultimate reality, and the refreshing libation is the sacrifice to the ancestors, the propitiatory offering of portions of food is for the disembodied spirits, and the revering of guests is the sacrifice to men.*
>
> *He should offer a guest, as soon as he arrives, a seat, some water, and food that has been ritually prepared and perfectly cooked to the best of his ability. This is Manu's Law.*

'Oh! It's you,' Govind said, when he saw Patrick.

18 Truth

Jhoti was right. Patrick knew it. He should never have come.
He would have turned and run – gone as far away from that
village as he possibly could – but his presence had caused more
of a stir in the village than the wedding. A white face hadn't
been seen in the district since the British left after Independence and, wherever he went, he found himself at the
centre of an entourage of farmers and children; the farmers –
especially the older ones – wanted to reminisce about what
had suddenly become 'the good old days', and the children,
flocking about him like hungry sparrows, wanted to try him
out with snatches of English and beg for any kind of souvenir
he could extricate from his pockets. Govind treated him as
the honoured guest and, for a day at least, Jhoti and her
relatives lavished attention on him.

But he should have left. Unreasonable bitterness welled
up inside him. Why hadn't he acted sooner? And how could

she go and allow herself to be married off for someone else's convenience? His anger at himself, and her, grew and grew.

He and Marvinder came face to face just once. After the wedding ceremony. He had watched her father give her away, and watched the four-times circling which bound her to the schoolmaster; then, when she and her husband were seated on their thrones to receive their guests, he came before her with head bowed, his pain and anger flooding out.

'So this is your truth and beauty, is it?' he murmured cruelly, unable to hold back the bitterness.

'It is truth. I hope the beauty will come,' she whispered.

In his head, he was begging her. Take my hand, Marvinder. Run. Run. Let's go. We could do it. Run away from this place. Go anywhere in the world. You don't belong here. You belong with me. You could come with me. Now. We could just get out of here and never come back. We could be together for ever.

And her silent reply was, I love you Patrick, but the truth is, I have no choice. I have made my pledge. I'll never forget you.

Sparks from bonfires spewed up into the night sky, dazzling the stars with their bright golden spray. And as the goat boys and farmers sang in the flickering firelight about Heer and Ranja and about Lord Krishna flirting with the milkmaids, and of the eternal love he had for the beautiful Radha, Patrick gathered up his bag and fled into the night. Defiantly, he returned to the palace, plunging through the undergrowth, yelling out to the unknown owner. 'Yes, it's me! I'm back to pick your pathetic roses and sleep uninvited in the courtyard of your rotten old palace. Do what you like. I don't care. Tomorrow I'll be gone – and you'll never see me again.'

And the beast, who had watched it all from the ramparts, howled with all the rage and despair of the world.

19 Farewells

'Brother!'

Nazakhat turned at the sound. No other word was so beloved. 'Bhai.' No other syllable had the capacity to express total friendship, an unbroken pact and complete commitment, as this one simple word.

Jaspal came and stood at his side on the shore of the lake. He was wearing a saffron-coloured turban – the colour of sacrifice – and Nazakhat knew this was to be a farewell.

'Bhai!'

'You're going away, aren't you?' murmured Nazakhat. He stared hard at the lake, deep as his sense of loss, and wondered how he would ever numb the pain.

'I must. Don't you see, I must.' Jaspal spoke more like a man than a boy.

'Why? Why?' Nazakhat had wanted to be calm, but he couldn't prevent the words tumbling from his mouth. It's not that he hadn't known something like this was coming. He had felt a gulf opening between them – wider and wider. He had tried to hang on to their friendship. He would have done anything for Jaspal: cut off his right hand for him; die for him. But this – Jaspal's cold withdrawal, as if he was slowly turning to stone – this, Nazakhat had not been unable to understand. If they could have quarrelled, fought, brought their friendship to an end in anger and hatred, it would have been easier to bear. He was just floating away and Nazakhat could not find the means to bring him back. All he could do was watch as the gap between himself and Jaspal, his only friend, his blood-sworn brother, widened and widened so that all he was left with was the question, 'Why?'

'You were already torn from your home once,' Nazakhat reasoned desperately. 'After all the trouble it took you to come back to your village from England and find your mother, why should you want to leave again? You have everything! Everything!' His words sharpened with accusation. How could Nazakhat not feel bitter when he had lost everything? 'And don't your mother and father need you even more, now that your sister is married and gone?'

'It's just something inside me,' said Jaspal. His voice was hard, as if he feared that any softening might make him change his mind. 'I have to go; things I have to do – which can't be done here; things which I want to learn and can't be learned in the school I go to now. My people have been wronged,

Nazakhat, and I'm going to help to put it right.'

'Haven't we all been wronged?' Nazakhat asked, startled by the burst of aggression in Jaspal's voice. 'Can't I go with you?'

'You?' Jaspal looked him in the eye for the first time.

His face expressed more than any words. 'You? You – a Muslim? Go with me?' Nazakhat read it all – and suddenly realised that the gulf between them had widened too far.

Nazakhat held up his right hand in salute. 'Goodbye then. Brother.'

Govind and Jaspal took the train into Amritsar. Father and son sat inside on the wooden benches of a second class compartment, and didn't say a word to each other the whole journey. From the railway station, they made their way to the bus station. The bus was packed with farmers, wives, infants and bundles returning to their villages with the proceeds from their market sales in the town the previous day. Govind and Jaspal sat upright and squashed together on the long back seat, and stared at the road ahead, as separate from each other as if they were on other sides of the globe. They sat for three hours – travelling through oceans of fields; then suddenly a row of shacks, and they were there.

Only the two of them got off. The bus roared off leaving them in a cloud of dust. They didn't need to ask for the gurudwara. They could see it. Fixing their eyes on a brilliantly white dome, they left the main road and took a track which immersed them in wheatfields. Then there it was – about half a mile away, like a swan on the deep green of the fields.

Men and boys lounged around in the archway of the entrance, lean and bare-legged, wearing light brown tunics which fell mid-calf, with holster straps across their chests and the hilts of knives glinting at their hips; some held spears. Their turbans were mainly indigo, saffron or white; one or two wore black. They looked up with only mild interest as father and son approached.

'Is Amarjit Singh to be found?' Govind addressed one of the older men. The man nodded and waved his spear at a young boy – younger than Jaspal. The boy sped away. Jaspal and his father stood silently. No one spoke to them and they didn't speak to each other.

After some moments, the boy reappeared. 'Come,' he said. Jaspal and his father followed. They went down a verandah with a colonnade of pillars which cast sharp black shadows standing like sentinels. Off the verandah were doors, doors, doors and more doors. Some closed, some open – but those that were open had curtains, which flapped listlessly in the slight breeze, allowing them only glimpses of dark interiors.

The boy stopped before one of the doors, which was open, and pulled aside the curtain. It revealed a gloomy, smallish, square room, but with walls that rose ten feet high. A large bed took up most of the space and, above their heads, alcoves and shelves full of boxes stacked all the way up to the ceiling.

Amarjit was gossiping to another man while a number of young boys hovered near by.

'Ah! You've come!' he said approvingly.

'Sit.' He motioned them to a narrow bench. Govind and Jaspal obediently sat. 'Will you have buttermilk?' Govind nodded and Amarjit waved a hand. A boy disappeared into an inner room. After a while he returned carrying two metal bowls. He pulled up a table and placed the bowls before the father and son. Then he disappeared again. This time he came back with a large bucket of milk and a ladle. He scooped buttermilk into the bowls. Govind murmured thanks and the two of them drank. Another boy came and placed a bowl of gelabees on the tables. They ate in silence. Amarjit Singh just watched them.

When they had eaten and drunk, he beckoned them to follow him. The light outside was blinding after the dimness of the room. Govind and Jaspal followed the man up some steps to an upper room. Here an elder sat before a large book. His grey-bearded old face was severe as he peered through metal-rimmed spectacles at a book before him, which he didn't stop reading when they came in. Amarjit simply said, 'Sit and wait till he is ready to speak to you.' Then he left them. Once more, they sat on a bench and waited in silence.

Fifteen minutes passed. The elder read, occasionally grunting and bowing his head. At last he stopped and set the book aside, still open. He beckoned Jaspal. Jaspal stood up and took a step towards the old man. The elder looked at him – his eyes steely cool as they surveyed him from beneath grey bushy eyebrows. He picked up the book and handed it to him. 'Read,' he said.

Read. The word hung in the air like a stone defying gravity; heavy – yet suspended. Jaspal read.

'Hail, all hail to the True Guru, the Perfect,
Who hath grasped the Highest Truth!
On encountering the Guru, every thirst is slaked.'

Then the elder addressed Govind. 'Are you the father of this boy?'

'Yes, I am.'

'Do you give your consent to hand over your parental rights to the elders of the taksal, and from now on for this boy to come under the jurisdiction of the taksal, obeying its rules implicitly?'

Govind looked at Jaspal. He had never been a father to him. Now if he handed him over, he never would. Suddenly, more than anything, he wanted to grab his hand and rush back home to their village. 'May I have a few moments alone with my son?' said Govind standing up. The elder nodded his assent.

Govind led Jaspal out on to the upper colonnade. They

walked all the way round, noting how far away from anywhere this gurudwara was. How far from home – how far from normal society. 'Oh, my son! Is this really what you want? I know I have wronged you – wronged you all – your mother and sister; I know I've been harsh. Times have been hard for you and for all of us. But won't you forgive and let us try again? Give me the chance to be a better father?'

Jaspal made no comment. Gave no look. Stood like stone.

'Perhaps the school was not good enough for you. But this doesn't have to be the answer. You can change your mind. Come away. Go to the Khalsa College in Amritsar – at least it's in the town; at least we could see you; you could come home. Do you realise how your mother will miss you – especially now that your sister is married?'

'What do you care about my sister?' Jaspal's words were harsh.

'So your mind is made up,' said Govind woodenly.

'Yes,' said Jaspal.

'Then let us proceed with the interview,' said Govind and he walked back into the room. 'I give my consent for my son to be fully under your jurisdiction.'

'And will you donate one tenth of your income each year towards the upkeep of the gurudwara and the education of your son?' asked the elder.

'I will.'

It had seemed so long since Jaspal had looked right into

his father's face and into his eyes. He looked up now to make his farewells. Tears streamed from Govind's eyes.

Jaspal bowed low and, kneeling down, touched his father's feet with his head. Briefly, he gripped his ankles and then stood up, his head still bowed. When finally, he raised his eyes, Govind had gone.

20 The track of the wind

A tornado is a rapidly revolving column of air in touch with the ground.

There are some who live in the past and take on the wrongs of history, and make it their bounden duty to right those wrongs, even when the wrongs have been forgotten. For them, the future is nothing but following in the track of the wind as it swirls round the planet, sometimes building up to such a ferocity that it destroys all in its path.

'Is that the one you mean?' asked a senior priest. He looked down from the verandah at a class of boys learning the art of wrestling. About twenty boys worked in pairs; they tussled and kicked and weaved and swerved; first attacking by wrenching the arm and tripping the ankle, then, as they rolled on the ground, each trying to defend himself against the other, through strength and cunning and swiftness and surprise.

The man he spoke to didn't move, and it was hard to tell what he looked at from within his strange sunken eyes. A slight twitch in his jaw as he clenched and unclenched his teeth, was the only indication that there was a life and energy in this rock-like body – so gaunt, so sheer – shaved to edges, as if the bones of his frame had been sharpened into weapons.

Yet there was no question at whom they looked. One boy stood out; a boy who moved like Hanuman, the Monkey God – using his powers to duck and dive and reach and crouch; as if he made himself bigger and smaller, visible and invisible; such a boy was more than a warrior – he was a living weapon as much as an arrowhead or a spear or an axe.

'Yes,' said Amarjit Singh. 'That's him.'

Grunts and cries of pain rang round the courtyard, then came a shout of triumph. 'You are dead! Face it! I could have killed you if I had chosen. Concede defeat!'

'Dead, dead, dead, dead!' chanted all the other boys, forming an excited circle round the struggling pair.

A boy lay twitching and jerking on the ground, his face in the dust, while, kneeling over him, the other had both arms of his opponent pinned behind his back, and sat on the boy's knees so that he could not move his legs. The victor suddenly grabbed his opponent's turban and forced his head backwards. If he had kept going he could have broken his neck.

'Hey, Jaspal!'

A voice rang out fiercely across the compound. Pooran Singh, the music tutor, came striding across to them. He dragged Jaspal off his choking partner, who struggled to his feet, spitting the dust from his mouth.

'You hooligans! What are you trying to do?' demanded Pooran, grabbing each by the scruffs of their necks.

'He was going to kill me, sir! He was going to kill me!' spluttered the other boy.

'What rubbish!' exploded Jaspal. 'I only wanted to show him that I could kill him if I wanted to. Isn't that what you always taught us: to have the skill to fight and the control to judge? I wanted to prove I now have both.'

'See what I mean?' said Amarjit Singh.

'I do indeed,' nodded the senior with approval.

Aware that they were being overlooked, Pooran Singh whirled round and stared up at the two men on the upper balcony. He thrust the two boys apart and sent them to their quarters and dismissed the rest. Then he went racing up the stone steps to confront his fellow priests.

'Why did you let it go so far?' Pooran yelled angrily. 'Why didn't you stop it? That boy, Jaspal, was within an inch of killing Dalip – and you were just standing there letting it happen!'

'Arreh, brother!' Gurdev, the senior, soothed him. 'Don't

be so namby-pamby. Of course the boy wouldn't have killed him. He's not stupid. That's evident. Only a fool would go too far – and this boy is no fool. We trusted him and we were right to trust him. It wasn't you who saved Dalip, it was Jaspal, who knew when to stop. You would have stopped him too soon – and that would have been foolish.'

Pooran Singh stood silently at the rebuke of the older man. He glanced at the younger one next to him, silent and taut as a stalking predator, and felt a shudder of fear. He had never liked Amarjit Singh. The man was arrogant, cold, articulate yet uncommunicative. No one ever really knew what he was thinking. Pooran wasn't sure what Amarjit was doing in a temple, for never once in the three years that he had been here had he observed the love of God in him. He had watched him at prayer and watched him reading the great books, yet, it was as if he only went through the motions. There was no spirituality or commitment. More natural to Amarjit was when he was training his body, doing target practice either with a rifle or a spear, and spending hours in physical exercise. He wondered why Amarjit wasn't in the army. It would surely have suited him better.

He looked to the older man – the senior priest – for support. But the old man merely stared back with a look of such defiance that Pooran backed away with a shrug, briefly clasped his hands together with a respectful bob of the head, and retreated.

Pooran descended to the courtyard. He didn't look up, though he was aware of the malevolent eyes of the two men on him as he entered the prayer hall of the gurudwara. He crossed the cool tiled floor to some narrow steps in the far corner, which led down to a chamber beneath the holy dais on which the Guru Granth Sahib was read. It was a totally windowless room, lined completely – floor, walls and ceiling – with tiles and marble, so it had the coolness and darkness of a tomb, except that one single flame from an oil lamp burned on a low altar. It was here that anyone could come who needed absolute peace and tranquillity to meditate.

Pooran was disturbed. He bowed before the shrine and then sat on the hard floor, cross-legged. He had been feeling uneasy for a long time. Something was going on in this gurudwara which he couldn't quite grasp. There were questions he wanted to ask, but didn't know who to ask. He was aware of division – yet unsure who was divided from whom. It involved Amarjit Singh and the elder priest Gurdev, of that he was sure. He disliked the influence Amarjit had over the boys – especially those keen on the martial arts. There was always a cluster of young ones around him, seeming to like nothing better than to hear about the latest arts of combat. But Amarjit was a captivating storyteller. Pooran himself had been moved on many a monsoon evening, when Amarjit could hold a room enthralled with tales of the Afghan invasions or the heroism of Sikh saints and gurus such as Guru

Gobind Singh and Baba Deep Singh. But, there was something sinister about the way Amarjit used his powers of storytelling to inspire the young boys to fight and look for ways in which they could prove their prowess and heroism. He could make them yell for the blood of their enemies whether they were Afghans, Muslims, Hindus or the British.

In particular, Pooran had watched Jaspal. The boy had grown taller in the eight months since his father had left him in the hands of the taksal. As he stood there, all of five foot eight and growing, Pooran had already noted the steely muscles of the boy's limbs; the upright body; the head — mobile, watchful, listening, turning independently, like the head of a hawk, ready to swivel back to catch out anyone who approached from another direction.

Pooran knew this boy was special, not just because of the way he performed in his classes, but because of how he used his spare time. Where the other boys liked to congregate with their elders, to gossip and relax, Jaspal carried on training, as if what he learned within the class was not enough. He carried on perfecting yoga positions; after drill, he went on exercising his body; or, somewhere on the edge of the forest, he would continue to throw his spear, and practise his sword fighting positions. His scholarship, too, was above reproach. No one knew the scriptures better than he — and there was an intensity and fervour about the way that he sang hymns which could bring tears to the eyes of his dim-sighted teacher.

But Jaspal was unique in another way and Pooran was sure Amarjit had noted it too: the deadly coldness in the boy's eye, his nails bitten down to the quick, his lip chewed raw with some kind of inner rage. Such a boy could fight for causes. He could be a tool for the ambitions and dreams of others. Sacrifice appealed to him; he often fasted – and Pooran knew he was capable of starving for a purpose. There were certain people who harboured secret ambitions – great goals which they were prepared to fight and die for. With Jaspal on their side, what a weapon they would have; what a burning hope that their goal would have more chance of being realised.

'Wake up! Wake up!' the voice hissed urgently into his ear.

Jaspal rolled over with a groan, but then in an instant was awake, swinging his legs out of bed and reaching for his knife.

Amarjit liked that. He straightened up with a slight smile. 'Get dressed; bring your knife and spear; we're going out on a night manoeuvre.'

Before Jaspal could ask any questions, Amarjit moved on and awoke four other boys out of the twenty who slept in long rows. One of the four was Dalip.

Silently, the group led by Amarjit left the gurudwara and took a track across the fields towards a distant edge of the forest.

They walked in disciplined silence for half an hour, one

behind the other, following the bobbing kerosene lamp which Amarjit carried. When they got into the skirts of the forest, they walked a further twenty minutes, till, suddenly, Amarjit brought them to a halt with an upheld hand. In a small, circular clearing among the trees and undergrowth, they could see and hear an animal struggling and snorting and wrenching at its tether.

The boys drew into a close cluster with each other, alarmed by the sound of an animal.

'What is it?' they whispered.

Amarjit moved towards the sound holding his lamp high. It reflected into furious, demonic eyes, glowing red in the darkness.

How much light there can be in the darkness of the night. Above were the stars, piercing pinpricks of light; and the moon – a gibbous moon that night, hunching over the land, pouring down its light. And in the darkness of the undergrowth, there were other lights too – the glow-worms and fireflies, and the liquid eyes of boys, wide as pools as gradually they realised they were looking at a huge pig.

'This is a practice,' announced Amarjit. He no longer whispered, as it was certain that there was no one around to hear. 'You will each wrestle with this hog – as if your life depended on it. It is no soft animal this. Nothing fights with more ferocity than a pig, but you will not kill, unless I give the order. Do you understand?'

The boys nodded eagerly, a tremor of excitement rippling through them as they looked at each other challengingly. They had been taught about death. Their favourite stories were about death – it was the final test of all sacrifices – yet how far away death had seemed to them. Now they were going to be faced with it and it sent blood racing through their veins, and adrenalin pumping energy and fervour into their hearts. There was no fear. They were gods after all – and immortal.

Amarjit hung the lamp from the branch above the pig, where they saw it better now. It was imprisoned on a short tether and pawed the ground, grunting with furious resentment. There was a gasp from the boys as Amarjit strode forward and unlooped the tether.

The boys fell away with alarm, thinking he had freed it, as the pig rushed forwards like a cannonball. But then, before it reached the edge of the clearing – about ten feet away – it was jerked from its feet by the longer tether around one of its back legs, which neither the pig nor the boys had known was there. For a moment it rolled about squealing horribly, then it struggled to its feet, lunging to the right and left, charging round in a circle and then being jerked off its feet again, as once more it tried to escape to the forest.

When the boys realised that the pig was still a prisoner, they advanced again, tentatively, till they stood just a fraction out of reach. They looked to Amarjit. What now?

'You, Mohan!' Amarjit pointed at a boy. 'Grab the animal

and control it. Try and get it back on the short tether. Go now. Go, go, go!'

The other boys, at first silent with the task before them, began to chant too. 'Go, go, go!'

The boy stepped forward. He was on the far point of the circle from the pig. He prowled round trying to get behind the animal. But suddenly, the creature, aware it had been targeted, whirled round and faced Mohan. Mohan stopped and changed tack. He picked up a stick and hurled it. It struck the pig on the side and made it twist away. Mohan rushed forward and dived on to the pig's back, clasping his arms round its thick neck, groping for the rope. But almost instantly, the pig shook itself with such force that the boy was hurled to the ground.

Amarjit dragged the boy away and at the same time pointed at another to go in. This time Ranjit moved forward. He decided to face the pig. He stared at it aggressively, as competing warriors do; he stared right into its small red eyes, challenging it to a fight. He approached, crouched over, both arms in front as if wanting to embrace it, he edged closer and closer, murmuring soft words. The pig stood still watching him narrowly. The boy stretched out a hand – it was both in defence and an invitation to the pig, daring it to attack. The pig shuffled its odd little hooves and once again, pawed the ground, but its eyes never left the boy's face. Ranjit was close now, almost close enough to make contact. He gathered his energies, his muscles taut like fully wound springs, as he prepared to pounce on the pig and clasp its snout. He had worked it out when he was watching Mohan. It was the snout he must fasten on to like a vice.

But even as he thought his plan through and was about to put it into practice, the pig charged him. Wham! Right in the centre of his stomach. The boy fell winded to the ground. The pig turned ninety degrees almost on the spot, rushed back with a frightful scream, and headed the boy as he lay there gasping for air, opening and shutting his mouth like a landed fish. Amarjit grabbed the tether and tugged with all his might, dragging the pig from the boy, but not before the creature opened its jaws and took one revengeful bite into Ranjit's cheek. The boys rushed in and hauled Ranjit, bleeding profusely, out of the arena. It was all over in seconds. The pig galloped away, triumphant, till, once more, it was brought to its knees by the tether.

Now who? Jaspal and Dalip, looked at each other. Dalip held up a hand to Amarjit. 'Me, me! Let me go in next!' He longed to prove himself and wipe away the humiliation of having been trounced earlier by Jaspal. Amarjit gave him the nod.

Dalip didn't just rush in. He backed away into the shadows of the trees. The pig looked around. Who next? It snorted and pawed and paced; it suddenly raced round the circle, got tangled up in the rope and was brought to its knees. With incredible intelligence, it unwound itself and took up the defensive position, looking around it. Dalip still stayed in the shadows, but was moving silently round till he was behind the pig. That was always the best strategy. Mohan had got it partly right. Get it from behind. Dalip had once seen a leopard attack a buffalo. The image was imprinted on his mind. Like the leopard, he watched, taut, motionless, silent. The pig came to a standstill – all its senses strained, trying to work out from which direction the attack would come. It waved its snout in the air, sniffing out its attacker. Amarjit and the boys stood motionless with expectation. A strange silence hung over the forest; if monkeys fidgeted in their sleep, or nightjars and owls fluttered and hooted, they didn't hear it. Their eyes were fixed on the pig. Its powerful sides heaved, pumping the air through its great engine of a body, filling it with deadly energy. Where was Dalip?

When he came, he came like a rocket. Dalip hurled himself at the pig's rear quarters. The other boys retreated with shock, then lurched forward again, as the pig and the boy crashed to the ground.

'Yes, yes, yes!' the other boys chanted with delight. 'You've got him! Hold him! Go on Dalip, catch him, tether him. You can do it!'

Dalip hung on to its back legs, clawing for the short tether, but with no further strategy to see him through. The pig was hurling itself about, squealing and shrieking like the devil himself. With a sudden fierce movement, it twisted its head and managed to get its jaws over Dalip's arm. With a howl of pain, the boy let go. The pig got to its feet, charged round in a circle and then, with lowered head, thundered down on its victim.

There was a cry of alarm from the onlookers. Amarjit grabbed the rope.

'Now me!' cried Jaspal. 'Now it's my turn. Let me try!'

Amarjit shook his head and tugged the rope to drag the pig away from the fallen boy, but suddenly he was tugging on air; the rope broke and sent him tumbling backwards.

The pig, not quite realising it was free, ran first towards the group, then back to the boy. It pounded right up to Dalip, writhing on the ground, and stood astride him, then it lowered its snout towards his neck.

Amarjit got to his feet and grabbed his rifle. He unclicked the safety catch and was about to aim, when there was a muffled cry. A boy hurtled out of the darkness and scooped up the fallen rope. He flung himself bodily at the rear legs of the animal. The pig crashed sideways. The boy clasped his legs round its belly, while he wound the rope round and round its back legs. One arm now grabbed an ear and pulled its snout round to him, while the other hand stretched up, gathering force and hung suspended for a second in mid-air, before plunging downwards into its throat. A fountain of something black and sticky arched four feet into the air and sprayed the onlookers.

Jaspal stayed, clasped in that deadly embrace until the animal had stopped jerking and twitching – it seemed an age before it was completely still. Exhaustion and elation swept over him. He rolled off the vast animal and lay on his back, staring up at the moon, his knife still clenched in his hand.

Amarjit strode forward, rifle in hand and glared down at the boy in fury. 'You disobedient wretch.' He kicked him. 'I could have killed you, you idiot. And who gave you the order to kill the pig? Did I give the order? You'll never make a soldier till you learn to obey, do you hear!' He waved the other bedraggled and injured boys into line. They moved slowly and bewildered, aghast by what they had seen.

Dalip turned hesitantly to Jaspal to stretch out a helping hand.

'Fall in, Dalip. You owe him nothing,' snapped Amarjit Singh and he signalled them to follow him marching back to the gurudwara, leaving Jaspal still prostrate on the ground with a pool of blood from the dead hog gathering around him.

21 The lesson to be learned

For the rest of the month, Jaspal was banned from the martial arts classes and was sent to help in the kitchen by Amarjit, determined to teach him a lesson in discipline. At the midday meal, some weeks later, Jaspal was a server. He carried two buckets, one of dal and the other chapattis and moved along the line of hungry villagers and travellers who had called in for a free meal. He didn't look into their faces as, bent double, he paced his way down the line scooping a ladle of thin gruel on to their plates followed by a chapatti tossed into their open hands.

'Ahh! It's you!' growled a voice that particular day. A steely hand gripped Jaspal's ankle, halting him dead in his tracks.

Jaspal raised startled eyes to find himself looking into the face of his old nihang.

'My! You're a sight for sore eyes.' The nihang gazed in admiration at his protégé, standing so tall in his light brown tunic and turban the colour of marigolds.

'Followed my advice then, did you?' he cackled toothlessly.

'Hey! What are you doing here? It's good to see you!' To his amazement, Jaspal found himself choked with emotion. He wanted to embrace the old man, but instead just plonked down his buckets and knelt before him with clasped hands. Not for one moment, until then, had he felt homesick – not all the time that he'd been away from home, yet, seeing the nihang overwhelmed him with memories of belonging; memories of what it's like to mean something special to someone, in a way that you are with family or special friends, to be loved as a brother, son or friend. Not that the nihang was any of those things – yet the time they had spent together had created a bond in Jaspal and he looked at the old man with love.

'How long are you staying?' he asked.

'Oh, just tonight! I'm on my way to the Himalayas.'

'Only one night?' Jaspal was dismayed. 'Can't you stay longer? There won't be time to talk otherwise.'

'What on earth is there to talk about?' demanded the old

man scornfully. 'You are where you should be, and I am where I should be. There's nothing between us.'

Jaspal bent his head till it was touching the nihang's feet in total subjugation. 'Take me with you,' he said impulsively. 'I've had enough of this place. I've learned everything I need to know. Take me with you. I'll serve you and be your pupil. I've still never met another teacher who taught me as well as you. Please.'

'What can I do with you – just a stripling still wet behind the ears?' sneered the old man, contemptuous as ever.

'Jaspal! Get on with it! There are people hungry. Don't keep them waiting,' the voice of one of the priests rang out across the eating area.

'You heard him!' the nihang muttered bluntly. 'Get on with it. It seems to me there's one lesson you'd better learn, though to be honest, I thought you'd learned it even before we met – have no attachments. If you have attachments you care too much about worldly things. You can't be God's tool if you have attachments. Does my spear have attachments? Does he love me? Need me? No. He is a tool, waiting to be used by me and I in turn am a tool of God, waiting to be used. I have no attachments, not to anything nor anybody.' The nihang bent his head and began to eat his dal and chapatti.

Jaspal paused. He understood, but the pain pierced his soul. 'Goodbye then,' he said. His voice pleaded for a friend's farewell, but the old nihang wouldn't look up; wouldn't speak.

'Well, goodbye then,' repeated Jaspal and, picking up his buckets, moved on mechanically down the line.

'Hey! Give us more than that,' a voice beseeched him when he was near the end of the line. 'I've been walking for days with barely a few berries to keep me going.'

But Jaspal was hardly listening. He was watching his old nihang walking slowly towards the arch and to the outside world beyond. He put down the buckets. His inner soul cried out: wait for me! He was about to run and catch up with him, when the same voice berated him angrily. 'Do you hear me? More than that, you stingy young pup.'

The man who nagged him was one of a number of refugees that day. People from Sikh villages in the section of the Punjab which had become part of the newly created Pakistan were still trickling across the border. The stories they brought with them of brutality, murder and mayhem sent ripples of anger through the gurudwara. Jaspal saw that this man had severe injuries. A dirty, stained cloth bound a wound on his head and just a stump of a hand which had barely healed after amputation.

'What happened to you?' exclaimed Jaspal.

The man looked up at him pitifully, as if to say, how would you ever understand what happened to me? He shrugged and indicated more on his plate and, with his good hand, stuffed his mouth with chapatti. As Jaspal moved away, the man suddenly growled, 'What would you know about death? Only good for killing cockroaches, eh?'

'Cockroaches!' laughed Jaspal bitterly. 'I killed a pig – a great big fat pig. I slit its throat – and that's just a start.'

'A pig is a pig. Now a man is a different kettle of fish.' The wounded man looked up at Jaspal with narrowed, bitter eyes.

That night, after prayers, when the Guru Granth Sahib had been put away with ceremony and the singing of hymns, Jaspal hung around the edge of a group of villagers who were camping within the gurudwara that night, and listened to their talk.

The people said they had tried to stay in their villages over the border, and carry on living side by side with their Muslim neighbours as they had done for generations, but it was no use. There were people determined to drive away as many Sikhs, Hindus and non-Muslims as they could. One man's entire family was burned to death by a mob of youths who came with torches. When the man went to the authorities the next day, the police grinned and said, 'It's our aim to drive out every single Sikh from our country, except one – we'll need one for the zoo. Are you volunteering?'

'That's what they've been doing to us. The world seems to think it can do what it likes with the Sikhs. We get driven from pillar to post. The Muslims have Pakistan; the Hindus have Hindustan; we should have Khalistan – '

'I'm all for it, I tell you!' It was Amarjit Singh. He had stood up, his spear in one hand and a rifle in the other. His face shone with purpose and zeal. 'And we mustn't forget the enemy within. We should kick those collaborators out of the temples and put in our own lot. We need priests who believe in our gurus, our aims, our destiny.'

'Yeah!' A great roar of agreement filled the air. Men clambered to their feet, their knives drawn, their spears held high! 'Khalistan Zindabad! Khalistan for the Sikhs!'

Jaspal, too, leaped to his feet excitedly. His soul burned to fight for the cause. He hadn't felt like this since he had ruled his gang in London and led them into battle with their rival gangs.

'Let us form an army within.' It was Amarjit again, who was speaking. 'A sacred army in which every man is prepared to sacrifice his life if needs be. We will be like the brotherhood again! The five – but multiplied a thousand times. Who of you here would offer his head to me for the cause?' cried Amarjit, echoing the famous plea of the tenth guru, Guru Gobind Singh who, two hundred years earlier, had demanded proof of a willingness to be sacrificed. Everyone knew the story of how the Khalsa Brotherhood was formed. How, one by one, five young men volunteered to die for their leader just because he asked them to. Each disappeared behind a curtain, and the horrified onlookers saw the silhouette of the guru raising his sword and bringing it down on the victim. After each one, Guru Gobind Singh reappeared with a bloody sword and demanded the next volunteer. The crowd had been overwhelmed with fervour. That was true sacrifice, when men were prepared to die because their leader said so. When Guru Gobind Singh had convinced the crowd of his need for ultimate sacrifice, he flung back the curtain to reveal all five alive – and thus was the brotherhood formed.

'Blasphemy!' muttered a priest near Jaspal. 'The man speaks blasphemy, using that story to justify his ambitions.'

'Yes – he's dangerous,' agreed another voice, and Jaspal realised it was Pooran, the musician. 'Haven't we had enough of war and death? Didn't the first guru wish us to get along with our fellow Indians – Muslim and Hindu?'

'Who will join me? Who will form a sacred battalion to fight for our precious homeland?' Amarjit's voice had risen with passion. He stood taller than the rest who crowded round him – his face narrowed and hawk-like, his eyes burning with fanaticism.

'Me! Me!' Many voices called out – and Jaspal's was among them. He put distance between himself and Pooran. There should be no mistaking whose side he was on.

Pooran shook his head sorrowfully and held out a hand as if to say, Jaspal – think again!

But Jaspal turned his back and crawled to Amarjit's feet.

Suddenly, Jaspal realised that, crouching next to him in the darkness, also listening, was Dalip Singh – his rival.

'Huh! I don't know why Amarjit Singh bothers with teaching us how to slay pigs – when it's Muslims we should be slaying – and Hindus too. Now that would be a test. We should be hunting them out of our homeland. If I knew where to find one, I'd go right now and slit his throat.'

'You can't even overcome a pig,' sneered Jaspal. 'How could you kill a man?'

'OK, clever dick! I know you're stronger than me – a better fighter – but it takes all sorts. I've got guts – you can't deny that. And for this kind of battle, even the strongest can't fight alone. You and me – now we could be a team, couldn't we? I'd face up to any man as I did the pig – if I could lay my hands on an enemy. I'd show you.'

'I can lay my hands on one. I know where there's a Muslim,' hissed Jaspal softly. 'He brought dishonour on my family. It would be deserved even if he weren't a Muslim. But you're all talk, Dalip. I always thought that. Whatever your boasting, you wouldn't have the guts.'

'Try me!' whispered Dalip. 'Just try me.'

'All right!' Jaspal turned to him and thrust out a hand. 'You're on!'

22 The beast lay dying

When someone has done, is doing or is going to do an act of shame,
then he should know that it has the mark of the quality of darkness.
Manu's Law

The beast lay dying. She hadn't been to see him since her marriage. By day, he wandered the desolate ramparts of the palace and the wilderness garden but still kept vigil at the tomb, beating the drum the whole night long.

One day he stopped by the bush of white roses and picked one. He held it to the two holes, which were all that was left of his nose, and sniffed it. Then a great howl left his throat and he fell to the ground in an agony of sorrow – and there he lay for two days, having lost the will to carry on.

It is where Nazakhat found him. 'When the drum didn't beat, I came to see why,' he explained as he bent over the half-conscious creature. 'Why stay here? Let me take you to Pakistan.'

'This is my palace, my land, my home. It has been in my family for hundreds of years. No, I am dying, Nazakhat, and it is here that I wish to die. But I beg one thing of you. Bring her to me, just one last time. Let me see her sweet face and hear her voice? I beg you. Persuade her to come. It would be my greatest comfort and consolation.'

The beast couldn't bring himself to say her name – but it was to Marvinder that Nazakhat went and delivered the message.

Marvinder consulted her husband, Bahadur. 'If you disapprove, then I will not go,' she said.

Bahadur looked at Nazakhat's stricken face.

'Take her, Nazakhat. I will follow behind, but is only my caution and anxiety for her safety. I promise not to interfere.'

The palace seemed almost swallowed up in the deep lush wilderness. Nazakhat accompanied Marvinder an hour before sun down. She moved as if she were sleepwalking, saying not a word to Nazakhat on the way. Bahadur watched them ahead of him, feeling more like a father guarding his children, than a husband. He hadn't intended to love her when he married her, he had intended to honour her, treat her with respect and share his ambitions and ideals with her – and it had worked.

Already she had made a huge difference to the school. The children were willing to learn from her because they loved her. And now he realised, that he loved her too.

They reached the long avenue of trees which led from the lake up to the front terrace of the palace. The sun had already dipped to the level of the top terrace. Wonderful smells of lemons and ugli fruit, jasmine and orange blossom, began to gather in the cooling air. He would pluck some for her hair. But he wished they had left earlier. The shadows were deep, as if they gathered in waiting for the darkness to come.

When they reached the portico, Bahadur said, 'I'll wait for you down here in the courtyard.'

Marvinder nodded and gave a grateful namaste. Then Nazakhat led her through the lower chambers and to the steps which led down under the ground. She shivered suddenly, remembering the last time she had descended into the underground tunnels. 'Why did he choose to see me down here?' she whispered.

'Because he is too weak to climb to the upper terraces. He is dying, Marvinder. He wants to say goodbye.'

'Will you stay with me?'

'If you want.'

She nodded firmly that it was what she wanted.

They were gone a long time. The sun had dropped lower and lower, terrace by terrace. Bahadur roamed around restlessly. The silence disturbed him. He wished now he'd followed them inside just to know into which part of the palace they had gone. Now he wandered from chamber to chamber, and then began to climb the stone steps which took him up and up to the palace roof. At each level, he searched the rooms – but they were empty – smelling of emptiness; even his breath echoed with emptiness.

From the highest terrace, he gazed out across the dark expanse of the lake, gleaming under the last rays of the sun; sinking into the waters as the English twins had sunk all those years ago – watched from this very spot by Marvinder and their elder sister, Edith.

The singing, when it came, seemed to emanate from the stones of the palace; from the walls, from the floors beneath his feet. It rose and fell like a monsoon wind and encircled him with its strange echoing tones. He felt a terror that he couldn't explain. He began to descend the steps, faster, faster, all but stumbling in the dimming light. He wanted to follow the sound, knowing that that was where he would find Marvinder, but whichever direction he turned, the sound was always somewhere else. He ran from chamber to chamber, pressing his ear to the walls, yelling her name into the stones.

Then there was a light – and Nazakhat appeared carrying an oil lamp.

The beast lay on the couch – the same couch on which he had put out the wedding garments a year ago. He was out of the reach of the light. 'I am dying,' he said.

'I know,' Marvinder answered.

'God knows where my soul will go. I have the mark of darkness on me.'

Marvinder came closer. He held up a hand to shield her from his face, but she took his hand. 'I had an old teacher once, in England, who used to talk to me about truth and beauty. I never really understood it – though I liked the sound of the words. But now I know what it means. You have shown me. You have spoken the truth, even when it was horrible, and that has made you beautiful. You needn't ever hide yourself from me again.'

Still holding his hand, she bent down and kissed the smudge of his dark, featureless face as though she kissed the surface of the lake.

He burst out singing.

Bahadur and Nazakhat stood in a corner of the chamber watching.

When he had stopped singing, the beast said to Marvinder, 'This palace is now yours, and so too is part of the treasure which was my family's treasure. It is all yours. The other part is Nazakhat's. Just in this short time, he has been like a pupil and a son to me. So I have provided for him too, but I have told him to go to Pakistan. He is young and Pakistan must be his country now.'

Nazakhat came and stood near Marvinder.

'Dear children,' the beast murmured, 'you are divided by a sword not by God.'

His words had barely left his lips when the silver steel of a sword pierced the gloom. There was a rush of feet and a shriek of war cries.

'There he is!' cried a hoarse voice, itself breaking with fear and bravado. Two figures in black turbans and dark tunics, one with a sword, the other with a spear, sprang into the room.

'Kill the enemy!' they screamed and rushed over to the couch.

With incredible strength, the beast thrust Marvinder aside as Bahadur, too, plunged forward in desperation. The sword came down.

23 The second daughter: Beryl's story

Ohio,
USA
March 1960

Dear Granny O'Grady,
I would like to get in touch with my real father in India.
Now that Mom is dead, it makes me think about who my
relations are – especially as I have no real blood relations in
America. Ricky agrees with me. Even though Ricky is my
stepfather – he is the best dad a kid could ever want – and

it's not because I don't love him that I want to get in touch with my real dad. It's just something to do with understanding who I am exactly. It's strange having as much Indian blood in me as white blood — yet I don't know a single other Indian, and I know absolutely nothing about India or what it means to be Indian, and I figured that was like not knowing who half of me was.

So, Granny, do you have my father's address so that I can write to him? Ricky says he might take a year off next year, and he and I could travel to India — and that would be so so great.

Please write real soon.

Lots of love,

Beryl

PS Please say hi to Grandpa — and also to Patrick, Michael and Kathleen. Ricky says, if we go to India we would first take the ship to England and then another ship across to India. That means we could visit with you guys. Won't that be great?

The waiting was painful. Now that Beryl had made a decision to get in touch with her father, she was impatient beyond endurance. She watched the post every day — long before it was possible for a reply to come. Ricky said a letter might take three weeks to get there, then three weeks for a reply to come back. Beryl thought he might be exaggerating a bit so that the waiting wouldn't be so bad, but in the end it was over two months before a letter came – not from Grandma O'Grady, but from Uncle Michael.

Dear Beryl,

Mam asked me to write to you because she's been rather poorly recently and didn't feel up to it. Your mother's death was a terrible blow to her – especially as your gran had been saving up to come and visit her in America. We were all very upset. None of us expected never to see your mother again.

Our mam said she was surprised that you wanted to find your father, Govind Singh. We all reckoned he wasn't worth finding, especially after what he did to you and your mother. But we all discussed it and agreed you had a right to find him if you wanted. Our Kath – your Aunty Kathleen has been writing to Marvinder – your half-sister – so we have an address.

> *Mr Govind Singh*
> *Deri*
> *Batala District*
> *Punjab*
> *India*

I expect you realise that you also have a half-brother called Jaspal. A right tearaway he was too. He was bound to come to a bad end.

One thing made us very happy, that you would come to England first and see us. This would please our mam very much. She was always very fond of you – and it broke her heart when you and your mother went away to America. We would all love to see you, Beryl. Kith and kin have to stick together.

Hoping you get a reply from your father,
Much love from us all,
Uncle Michael

After Beryl got that letter, she went to her room and took out her mother's special suitcase, the one in which she had kept everything to do with England – all the letters and photographs and birthday and Christmas cards which had come over the years. She found a photograph taken at her O'Grady grandparents' twenty-fifth wedding anniversary. There was a picture of the whole O'Grady family, along with her mother, real father, Govind, and Marvinder and Jaspal.

She looked hard at each one – especially at Marvinder, Jaspal and her father. She looked at herself – at her baby face, aged three, laughing and stretching out her hand to the camera. But she was a stranger to herself in the midst of strangers. The only face she knew was her mother's.

Their faces were blurred – like her memory. She shut her eyes tightly, and tried and tried to remember something of when she had been three, living with her real father. Then she looked at the photograph through a magnifying glass – but it didn't help. Their faces told her nothing. Mostly, people just smile in a photograph, no matter what. Through the blur, that was the only thing you could see they were doing – smiling – except Govind. He wasn't even looking into the camera, but down at his feet – as though he knew that he shouldn't be part of the photograph.

Beryl sighed. From everything she had heard about her real father as she grew up, he shouldn't have been there in that photograph. She heard how he had lied to her mother when they married, and didn't tell her that he was already married with a wife back in India and two children, Marvinder and Jaspal.

After her mother died, Beryl talked all this through with Ricky. She wondered if she should see her father when he had been so bad. Ricky said he had been thinking about it for a long time – and he and Maeve had discussed the possibility that one day Beryl would want to know more about her real father and even visit him. Ricky reassured her. Maeve and he had both agreed that, no matter what Govind had done, he was her father.

Beryl stared at the dark face again. Ricky said the war had done funny things to people and that he may not be that bad. She realised he was quite handsome, so far as she could make out, and she wished and wished and even prayed to God, please make my dad not be that bad.

'Well, now you have an address, I guess you'd better get on with writing that letter,' said Ricky.

'Won't you write it for me, please!' Beryl beseeched him.

'You write it first, honey,' said Ricky gently, 'and I'll check it over and see that it reads OK.'

With a sigh, she took one more look at her father's face in the photograph and began to write: *Dear Dad.* 'Ricky?' she yelled, halted straight away by the word 'Dad'. 'Do I say Dear Dad? I mean he hasn't been my dad even if he is. Shouldn't I say, Dear Mr Singh?'

'You say what feels right, I think that's the only way. If it doesn't feel right to call him Dad, then don't,' advised Ricky.

She screwed up the piece of paper and started again. After she had done that three times, Ricky suggested doing it in rough first to save paper.

It took eight goes, before she came up with something that seemed right.

> *Dear Mr Singh,*
>
> *My name is Beryl Jansen. I am your daughter. My name used to be Beryl Singh when my mother was married to you. But when my mother found out that you already had a wife and family in India, she left you and came to America where she married my stepfather, Ricky.*
>
> *I expect you have heard the news that Mom died of cancer on 17 March.*

Even though Ricky couldn't have been a better father to me, now that Mom is dead I thought I would like to write to you as my real father. After all, we do have the same blood in our veins. Ricky agrees with me.

This photo shows you how I look now, aged nearly sixteen. I don't suppose you would recognise me, seeing as how you haven't seen me since I was three.

I would be really glad to hear how you are.

Please give my regards to my half-sister, Marvinder, and my half-brother, Jaspal.

Yours sincerely,
Beryl Jansen (Singh)

Ricky read it through and said it was fine. He found an envelope for it. They sent it airmail.

After Beryl posted it, she said she felt weird. She didn't want to let Ricky out of her sight, terrified he might abandon her. She thought, what if my dad doesn't want me either, or if he turns out to be gross – I'd have no one! If Ricky went out, Beryl would ask, 'When are you going to be home?' If he was vague – 'Oh, around five or six.' – she'd say, 'No, exactly when are you going to be home?' So he'd have to be exact: 'How about like five eighteen and sixteen seconds precisely?' he laughed.

But he understood. 'Don't worry kid. I'll never leave you. You would have to kick me out before I left you.'

'And you won't change your mind about going to India with me – even though it's to find my dad?' Beryl pressed him anxiously.

'No, honey. I won't change my mind. Anyways – I've always wanted to go to India. See all those tigers and rajahs and the Indian rope trick!'

A letter came at last. A thin, bloodless, pale pink letter in an envelope, so thin that Beryl could see the scrawly writing through it. It had a row of Indian stamps with Mahatma Gandhi's head on them, and was stuck down so tight, she didn't know how to open it without ripping everything. 'You do it,' Beryl said, giving it to Ricky. Ricky got out his Swiss army knife and selected his finest blade, and just managed to get the tip under one corner. Then he slit it open and held it out to her.

She didn't want to take it. 'You read it!' she begged.

Ricky spread the one spidery page out on the kitchen table and they leaned over it together.

> Dear Beryl,
>
> Thank you for your letter. I am very sorry to hear that your mother passed away. India is a long way for you to come, but if you ever reach my home, you would be made most welcome.
>
> Yours sincerely,
> Govind Singh

'Is that it?' Beryl was confused. 'Is that all my father has to say?' She burst into tears. 'That's it then. I'm not going. He doesn't want to see me. Look – you can tell. There's no invitation – he doesn't ask how I am – he doesn't even mention the photo I sent of me,' she stormed.

'Hey, hey! Hold your horses,' he soothed. 'This is a repeat performance for Govind, don't yer see?' Ricky explained. 'You were too small to remember, but your mom told me about it so many times – about how Jaspal and Marvinder just turned up out of the blue in England; kids he thought were far away in India whom he would never see again. Then boop! There they were on his doorstep, and tipped you and your mother's lives upside down. Now it's happening all over again. A child he thought he would never see again writes him out of the blue and says she wants to come and see him. We don't know what that's going to do to his wife – and his other kids. Don't you see?'

'I suppose . . .' Beryl muttered in a thick voice.

'Look, honey. Seems to me, he wouldn't have written back at all if he wasn't interested. Seems to me that even though he's scared – upset – embarrassed – you name it – he's also interested. You are his daughter. Read this again: "If you ever reach my home, you would be made most welcome." He wouldn't write that if he didn't mean it. No, in my opinion, we carry on with our plans. We'll send him another letter in a while when we know what dates we will be in India. We'll give him plenty of time to consider and send back a reply, and we must play it cool. OK, pardner?' He held out the flat of his hand.

'OK, pardner,' she grinned sheepishly through her tears and slapped the palm of her hand against his. They gripped and then hugged.

24 Of flesh and blood

15 September 1961

My Dear Marvinder,

Your half-sister, Beryl, arrived last week with her stepfather, Ricky. I had the shock of my life, I can tell you. I couldn't believe it at first – she looked just like you. I thought it was you standing there at the front door. Then I had to remind myself that you are now twenty-eight years old like me, and Beryl is sixteen – so it couldn't be you, though I'll bet you haven't changed much judging by the photograph you sent me of yourself last year.

We didn't know what they would be like, Beryl and her stepdad. We were all really nervous. Mam kept saying she wished Beryl wasn't coming – especially not with Ricky; that it would just stir up bad memories. She wanted to go away to Ireland and stay with my aunty, Bernadette. But me dad said wild horses wouldn't drag him over to Ireland, and if she went, who'd look after him? So she had to give up the idea. She was very moody about it, but we were all glad. Anyway, we told her plain. I mean – we said to her – 'Beryl is our own flesh and blood. What happened in the past wasn't her fault. We should meet her.'

We weren't too keen to meet Ricky at first, but, honestly, Marvi, they're both smashing. We all really like them. Mam took one look at Beryl and hugged the poor girl till she nearly suffocated, then Mam burst out crying calling Beryl her poor, little, motherless grandchild. She told her that she shouldn't be too upset without her mammie, because her mammie was up in heaven with the angels. She nearly got us all going. As for Ricky – well, I wouldn't have minded having Ricky for a dad, I can tell you. He's so handsome – I mean he looks like James Dean – well, a little anyway. Josephine said I was exaggerating just a little. Oh, all right, he's not like James Dean. His nose is stubbier and he's got curly brown hair. Josephine says it's ginger, but I think she's wrong.

They've booked a passage on the SS Orion on 10 October. They'll reach India by the end of the month – well, you'll know all that from Ricky and Beryl, because I know they've written and told you.

This is the first time I've ever wished I weren't married with nippers, because otherwise, I would have gone too. I know you and Beryl are half-sisters, but no one was ever more of a sister to me than you were. If only I knew we could meet again.

But — now — here's a surprise. Patrick turned up. He's been away for three years without leave — would you believe. I hope it means we'll see more of him. I think it's about time he married and settled down, don't you? Otherwise he'll turn into a fuddy-duddy. You know, I'll never forget the day when he heard about Bahadur's death. He was visiting us on leave, he went white as a sheet and rushed off to vomit in the bathroom. He told us all he'd picked up a tummy bug, but I got the impression he was — well — turned upside down by the news. He hadn't received the letter in which we told him. All he said was, 'Why didn't she write and tell me?' It was upsetting all that. I still shudder when I think about what you suffered. I keep expecting to hear you've married again. You should Marvi. It's not right for a young woman like you to be alone — and it's not as though you ever had any children.

Well, Marvi, I hope your school is flourishing. Fancy you being head of a school! Who would have believed it? It's amazing how you took on Bahadur's work. Remember school here? Perhaps I should send my little Tracey and Ian to you. We can't help wondering what became of Jaspal. You never tell us about him. We all felt terrible when we heard what he did.

I'll have to be patient for your next news. I know it will seem like eternity before Beryl and Ricky come back from India. But we've instructed them to take thousands of photographs with Ricky's posh camera.

Till then, take care, dear Marvi,

Tons and tons of love,

Kath

25 Sisters

When the train finally slid into Deri at a walking pace, four hours later than scheduled, leaning out of their open door and eagerly looking up and down the platform, Beryl and Ricky were almost shocked by the silence. After the bedlam of Bombay, and the raucous disregard station life displayed all the way to Amritsar, for the divisions between night and day, sleeping or waking, to arrive at a small, rural station, where bodies didn't instantly arise to bombard you with tea or food or toys or alms, was an unexpected surprise. The only living things to show any interest in their arrival were a thin, bony dog, a cabal of crows and a group of monkeys, who briefly paused in their scrupulous nit-picking and grooming of each other and then resumed it.

Even as they wondered if there was any human here, a portly stationmaster waddled out of an office, trying to tie the drawstring of his pyjamas while clutching a red flag and a green flag. Then, from behind the barrier, there emerged a young woman – and, in a flash, Ricky said, 'That's your sister!'

'It can't be,' Beryl stammered.

But Ricky bet a million dollars that it couldn't fail to be Beryl's sister. 'You're alike as two peas in a pod!'

Beryl laughed nervously. 'Don't be ridiculous. How can I possibly look anything like her!' She peered almost secretively from the train doorway at the slim, upright, beautiful woman who gazed searchingly up and down the train as the doors swung open, and a few passengers heaved themselves off with bag and baggage. Beryl felt very self-conscious and held back. 'I'm scared, Ricky.'

'Come on,' he commanded, and opened the door. As she and Ricky dropped down on to the platform with their rucksacks, looking like typical American backpackers – both of them in jeans and T-shirts – Beryl was overcome with how dumpy and spotty she must look, and with braces on her teeth. She felt such a lump compared to the woman Ricky insisted was Marvinder, who was wearing a soft cream tunic and pyjamas and a veil draped round her shoulders. Her hair was drawn back in a single neat bun and Beryl noticed how little jewellery she wore compared to most Indian women. Over an arm, she was carrying two garlands of flowers.

When the woman saw them, her face, which had been solemn – almost sad, broke into such a warm, loving smile, that all Beryl's anxieties were swept away. The closer she had got to seeing her father, the colder her feet had become, and she had driven Ricky mad by asking him almost every day, 'Do you think we were right to come? It's all going to be so embarrassing. And what about Marvinder and Jaspal? They might hate me. If you had a daughter from the past turn up, I don't think I'd like it, so why should they feel any different?'

'Honey,' Ricky would say, 'if they don't like us, we'll go away again. See? It's as easy as that. Stop worrying.'

Seeing Marvinder's welcoming face made her feel better, but it was still odd not knowing how to greet her – whether to give her a hug and a kiss or shake hands – or what.

But Ricky took over. He walked straight up to her and said with a friendly smile, 'Marvinder Singh, I presume?' and when she nodded yes, Ricky said, 'Meet your sister, Beryl.'

'Hi, Marvinder!' Beryl mumbled, blushing profusely.

Marvinder came forward and placed one of the garlands around Beryl's neck and then took both hands in hers and said, 'Welcome, sister, welcome to Deri.' She then put a garland round Ricky's neck and did a respectful namaste.

'Hey, Jungli!' Marvinder beckoned a strange, hunched-up figure in a vivid pink turban and white cotton shirt and trousers. 'Jungli will carry your bags,' she said.

Beryl wasn't sure if Jungli was a man or a boy – he moved so oddly – as if he hardly knew how to walk. But he was strong. He just yanked up both rucksacks – one on his head and one on his arm – and, the extra weight supposedly making no difference to him, bounded out of the station to a small hooded cart drawn by a little spindly horse.

'Come,' Marvinder said in a high, tinkling voice. 'We have a tonga waiting for you.' She led then towards the flimsy structure, which made Ricky and Beryl look at each other in some alarm, for it rocked like a boat as the rucksacks were stuffed inside.

'Are we meant to get in that?' Beryl whispered.

Marvinder pointed to the rear-facing seats. 'You sit there and I'll climb up next to Jungli,' she said confidently.

'Poor little horse!' Beryl couldn't help exclaiming. It seemed barely credible that this creature, all skin and bone, could possibly pull a cart plus four people and two rucksacks. But off it went, tripping along, the bells round its neck tring-tringing in time with its feet.

The white road stretched ahead of them, thin as a ribbon, wavering between the eucalyptus trees which cast frail, dappled shadows across their path. No one spoke. Ricky and Beryl stared with interest from the tonga at the passing scene; the abandoned, white, crumbling church, where buffalos were grazing in the neglected graveyard, the odd peeling bungalows with broad verandahs and thatched roofs, the large, empty compounds with barren flowerbeds, and the once green lawns turned to dust. A lemon tree glowed yellow and ghostly – as if some colonial child from another age had just sprung from a single swing which bobbed listlessly. Beyond were the low mud and brick dwellings of a village.

But they didn't go to the village. The horse suddenly veered off down a track and headed for a wilderness of great trees and undergrowth throbbing with crickets and birds fussing and fluttering.

'Goodness! What's that?' cried Beryl. 'Look, Ricky!' Emerging from the tops of the trees they glimpsed a vast building towering through the canopy, as though somehow a passing giant had picked up a chateau in Italy and dropped it in the middle of India.

'What's that?' echoed Ricky.

'It's the palace. It is now my school,' explained Marvinder, and they couldn't mistake the pride in her voice.

'What's a palace doing out here in the middle of nowhere?' asked Ricky.

'Two or three hundred years ago, a Mogul prince built it as a retreat for himself, to relax and go hunting,' Marvinder told them. 'In those days, there were many tigers. But then the British came; they defeated the princes, shot all the tigers and abandoned the palace. After partition, a descendant came back, wishing to die in his ancestral home. He came to know how much I loved his palace and, when he was dying, said it was his wish that I should have it. I turned it into a school. It had always been Bahadur's dream – that the palace should become a school. Alas, he never lived to see it happen.'

There was a momentary silence, then Ricky said gently, 'We are so sorry about Bahadur.'

'It was his karma – his fate,' replied Marvinder.

'And is my father there – in that palace?' Beryl asked nervously.

'No, my dear. He's in his own family home in the village. But I thought I'd bring you here first as you will both stay with me. This palace has many rooms. When you have washed and changed and rested, then I will take you to see him. OK?'

She said OK in such a sing-songy way that Beryl burst out laughing. The atmosphere between them lightened.

'OK!' Beryl mimicked, and Marvinder laughed too.

Govind came out on the verandah. He had said his prayers and bathed. He stretched out his arms and breathed deeply. The air was as warm as fresh buffalo milk, and he gulped it with special relish. Today was special. He was going to see his daughter. He extended his arms and his chest and inhaled long and deep. A thought sprang into his mind that in England he had never made this ordinary common gesture so familiar to Indians. Until now, he hardly thought about England at all, though he could never anticipate when a sudden flash would illuminate a memory or sensation: when the sound of a young child's laugh could remind him of his little daughter Beryl as sharply as an arrow shot from the bow. At such moments, Jhoti might have observed him give a little shudder or frown, or suddenly stare into space as though seeing something enacted before his eyes. Now Beryl was a young woman – and she was here in his own village.

Yet Marvinder, his first-born daughter, didn't mean anything to him at all. It wasn't the same – he didn't know why. Perhaps because, when she was born, no one rejoiced. Girls are a curse and no mistake. Yet it was Marvinder's strength and courage which had brought the family back together again across oceans – back home to their village. How quietly she had been a dutiful daughter. Even now that she was a widow, and running Bahadur's school, she still found time to join her mother serving him food, watching to provide for all his needs. Even this morning, it was she who had cooked and given him his tali of chapatti and dal. She placed it before him as usual, but he never even acknowledged her. Oh, he knew she was there. He was aware of her watching as he began to work the chapatti in with his right hand, deftly soaking up the dal and consuming it piece by piece. And when he was finished, she was on hand, ready with a jug of cleansing water to pour over his fingers, and into his cupped hand so that he could rinse round his mouth. Such actions would not be known to Beryl. 'Beryl,' he spoke her name out loud, and realised he hadn't spoken it for more than twelve years.

As if summoned, Beryl appeared, walking shyly towards the bungalow, she in her jeans and T-shirt, looking so

American and, alongside her, Marvinder. Even so, he gasped at how alike they were. Sisters.

He stepped down from the verandah and paused with uncertainty. Then slowly, he approached the two young women. Marvinder fell back and stopped. Beryl continued walking – and, suddenly, in a rush, she flung herself into his arms, and he held her and held her and held her.

26 On living and dying

When Brahma awakens the universe moves; and when he sleeps and his soul is at rest, then everything closes its eyes.

Beryl and Ricky stayed a long time in Deri. There was nowhere else they wanted to be. They all had so much to learn about each other.

'Didn't you play the violin, Marvi?' asked Beryl one day when they were alone together. 'Kathleen said you played at a concert and everyone said you should be a concert violinist! Why weren't you?'

Marvinder laughed, 'I think Kathleen was exaggerating.'

'I wanted to be a ballet dancer,' said Beryl pulling a face and spreading her arms. 'A great, big hulk like me – can you imagine? I used to go to Donna Maldonado's Dance Studio and learn all sorts of dancing: tap, rhythm, South American and ballet, though mostly I learned by watching. My best teachers were my mom and Ricky, with me watching them and copying everything they did. I loved it.'

'What, Maeve too? Did she dance?' cried Marvinder.

'Yes – it was all because of Ricky! Ricky had always been with shows – and revues. Only when he was out of work was he a plumber. He was a good dancer – some said like Gene Kelly – and he got lots of work. But there was always so much touring around, and he didn't like leaving Mom and me, and – well – they always said it started out as a joke, that he would teach Mom a few steps so that she could be in the shows too, but then he found she was really good.'

'That's one thing I do remember about Maeve!' cried Marvinder. 'I remember how much she loved to go dancing! She was really beautiful. Kathleen used to say she was like Rita Hayworth – with all that lovely red hair.'

'Yeah! I know. I wish I had it sometimes,' sighed Beryl. 'Anyhow, Ricky trained her and they began to do double acts. I kinda barged my way in. I didn't want to be left out. Of course Mom wanted me to be like Shirley Temple – all the moms did. Mine wasn't alone in twisting my hair into rags every night so that they came out in long corkscrew ringlets which bounced when I walked. Trouble is, with my dark skin and dark hair and deep brown eyes, I was never going to look like that golden-haired cherub – not in a million years. But I could dance. Miss Maldonado said I was quite talented. I really fell in love with ballet. Forget Shirley Temple. I'd like to have been like that wonderful Russian ballerina, Tamara Toumanova. She was dark. Why couldn't I be like her? When I told Miss Maldonado that my dream was to be a ballerina, she said, "Forget it, honey. You'd never get into a corps de ballet with that brown skin of yours. Stick to Latin. Cha-cha-cha!"

'It only half broke my heart. I had so much fun touring with my mom and Ricky. Ricky had got one of these caravanettes – a whole little house on wheels. I could have lived for ever touring about from one little town to another. It was tough going back to school in Ohio after a whole summer on the road – but it helped me bear those snotty kids with their teasing and poking fun.

'I was cute as a small kid, and one summer, when Mom and Ricky were on stage in some one-horse town in the state of Illinois, I was round the back aping their number. Mr Bouschik, the hall manager, saw me and straight off put me on stage the very next night, danging behind my Mom and Ricky. It brought the house down and, from then on, I got my own little bit to do. Ricky said he was able to up the fee because of me. I felt so proud – especially when he handed me a ten-dollar bill – crisp as an autumn leaf. "This is yours, honey! You earned it." I had no idea what to do with so much money. Mom said it was a good policy to keep some and save some. So I kept five and saved five – and did that ever since. I had the money to go to India.'

When Marvinder murmured sympathetically, 'It must have been so hard for you when Maeve died,' Beryl realised how much she still wanted to talk about her mother – and with someone else other than Ricky. She had found it was really hard to talk to people about her.

Death embarrassed people and most changed the subject as quickly as possible. Even though Ricky never ever minded her talking about it, sometimes Beryl felt they were both in too much pain to help each other. She shuddered when she remembered how, too soon after her mother died, she had said to Ricky, 'Well, I suppose I'd better go and look up my real father.' Throughout all Mom's long illness, Beryl never saw Ricky cry. But the moment the words left her lips, she could have bitten off her tongue. His face quivered and tears sprang into his eyes. He turned away quickly – but of course she had seen. 'I . . . I mean . . .' she had stammered with embarrassment. 'Now that Mom's dead, you won't want me around, will you?'

She told Marvinder about it, as they strolled along the shore in the cool of evening. It was always such a soft, gentle time, just when the sun was dropping through the sky, taking with it the fierce heat of the day.

'I didn't realise Ricky could love me too, like his own real

sure he felt the same as me. He looked around – as though she'd somehow slipped out of her skin for a few moments and he thought he would see her behind him; that somehow, she'd come back, and her eyes would open – those strange, green eyes, Irish eyes, Ricky always said. He must have thought her lips would open, that her pink tongue would come out and lick them – and her sing-songy Irish voice would say "Hi, honey!" But she didn't. She'd gone. She'd gone right away from her skin; from her body. Her slightly open eyes weren't seeing; her fingers weren't touching, or her ears hearing. She'd gone from everything that made her who she was. When I touched her and kissed her – it wasn't kissing her at all; just this cardboard cut-out.

'That's when I began to think about my real dad.'

By now, they were right round the far end of the shore, looking at the lights in the village flickering into life as the light of day was slowly extinguished. The palace looked black against the darkening sky. Flocks of parrots wheeled among the parapets and terraces. Marvinder took Beryl's arm and they walked on and on.

'I wish I could remember us all being together, Marvi. It's so strange to think there was a life before Ricky, when my mom, our dad, you and Jaspal and me – we all lived together as a family. Don't you think it's weird?' Then she said quietly, 'Does your mother mind me being here? She is so lovely and kind. I would hate to hurt her. I like her very much.'

'Just as my husband's death and your mother's death was their karma, so my mother sees everything that she does as her dharma – her duty. So do not concern yourself,' Marvinder quietly reassured her.

'It must have been the hardest for your mother, Marvi. All that time not knowing if you and Jaspal were dead or alive – and then finding out about me and my mom . . .' Beryl broke away from Marvinder's side and ran to the water's edge. She stared out across the surface where flights of sand martins flew, wheeling and darting and swerving in and out of the last gold-tinged shadows, and tiny winged bats merged with them, squeaking their welcome to the approaching night.

Beryl wanted to cry. She waited till she felt under control before asking a question which had been haunting her. 'Were we happy then, Marvinder, you and me, Govind and Jaspal – all of us living together in London? When I was three, were we all one big happy family?'

'No.' Marvinder said the word decisively. 'I don't remember being in a happy family. I don't remember either Maeve or Govind being happy. None of us were, because none of us were in the right place or with the right people. Even you, Beryl – such a small thing that you were – you weren't as happy as you should have been. Even babies can sense when there is unhappiness around.'

'I thought I didn't remember Jaspal,' said Beryl. 'But now I realise I do. I remember that he hated me.'

'I think Jaspal learned to hate when he was in England. He hated everyone,' Marvinder said, almost to herself. 'He was very unhappy; very, very homesick.'

'Is it really true that Jaspal killed Bahadur?' Beryl suddenly burst out. Then she clamped her hand to her mouth, horrified at her clumsiness. 'Oh, Marvi! I'm sorry! It's just that – well, no one ever talks about him. It's as if he doesn't exist, and I wondered . . . how can you forgive him for killing your husband?'

Marvinder froze. Beryl didn't know whether she would rage or cry. Then Marvinder spoke low and fierce. 'No, no, no – that's all wrong! Jaspal was led on; influenced by the other boy. Anyway, it was a mistake. They hadn't meant to kill Bahadur.' Her voice shook with passion. 'It was the old Muslim prince they were after – stupid boys; trying to play at grown-ups; trying to play at heroic patriotism for some non-existent state. Bahadur got in the way. If only he hadn't come. I had Nazakhat to protect me. It was all a bungling mess.'

Beryl glanced at Marvinder's face, trying to work out from her expression what her feelings must have been. Had she loved Bahadur? Beryl couldn't imagine not marrying for love.

'What happened to Jaspal?' Beryl asked. 'Will I ever see him?'

'He ran away. Escaped. He's been on the run – all these years. He must be with some of those extremists in the gurudwaras in the Punjab. To them, he would be a hero.'

Marvinder's voice held a tinge of bitterness.

'And has he never been in touch?'

Marvinder looked startled and then guilty. 'Yes. Sometimes. He knows he can trust me. He is my brother.'

'And he is my brother too,' Beryl said, as if trying out the sound of the words.

Marvinder smiled a deep, sad smile. 'Yes. He is your brother too.'

Ricky and Beryl stayed in India till January, travelling a little, but always coming back to Deri. Beryl saw her father every day. He treated her like a queen. At times, it was too much. He insisted on buying her jewellery and beautiful pieces of material which he would then get a tailor in the bazaar to stitch into salwaar kameez. He said he wanted to make up for all the years he hadn't been a father to her and he kept her by his side as much as he could. Yet she couldn't help noticing that he never treated Marvinder like that – nor her mother. It was as though there was a different set of rules for the way he behaved towards them. As time went by, it made her feel uncomfortable.

One day, Beryl said to Ricky, 'When are we going home?'

27 Letters from across the ocean

The long, white road materialised like a phantom through the pale rays of the early morning sun. Little shepherd boys, enveloped in thin shawls against the chill of the night dew, ran with hard, flat, bare feet behind herds of goats, prodding them with sticks to guide them towards the shrubland beyond the village. Feet and hooves churned up the dust, sending it drifting into a cosmos of light and particles, rising into the thorny arched shadows of babul and badam trees.

Jhoti was out early. She splashed herself at the pump, washing out her mouth and picked a twig of neem to chew as she climbed the dyke up to the road. She hardly considered that this road had defined her life since the day she was born, and would until the day she died. Everything she knew in life had moved up and down this road, and only twice had she ventured more than ten miles from it in any direction; once, on her desperate mission to Bombay to look for her children, and the other when she made one pilgrimage to the Golden Temple in Amritsar.

But her mind had travelled — had always travelled — far beyond where her body could ever go. And as she walked now, towards the abandoned graveyard of All Souls Church, her mind traversed land and sea, and so vividly, did she evoke images of those people who had come and gone that she felt like an eavesdropper, leaning into their conversations, peering over their shoulders to catch glimpses of faces and expressions and gesturing hands.

'Ah Jhoti! I never forget what good friends we were.'

The voice spoke wistfully inside her head. Jhoti did not look to her side. She knew that, as she walked, pale, tragic Dora, whose skin and hair and papery thin limbs had seemed to be conjured up out of the fine white dust eddying in the road, accompanied her.

'Jhoti, you were like my mirror image, working side by side with me; each of us pregnant together, having our babies at the same time, and our children growing up friends — as you and I were friends. I don't think I was ever happier in all my life, than in those years. I never really left, you know. How could I? Don't we have a tie with the earth from which our children were born, and in which two of mine now lie? Not one day goes by when I don't walk alongside you to the graves of my darlings.'

Jhoti knew that was true. It was not the first time she had felt Dora's presence as she walked to the churchyard. Sometimes, Dora told her which flowers would be nice to pluck that day to put on their grave; sprigs of lemon blossom, temple flowers, flame of the forest, bougainvillaea and hibiscus. But the one she loved the most, the one whose perfume would suddenly surround Jhoti as she walked, was the tube lily. Such flowers were harder to get – but in season, when the flowersellers brought them to the bazaar, Dora would plead with Jhoti to get them; and she did, holding them close to her nostrils as she carried them to the tomb.

'Beryl came to tea today,' Dora said inside Jhoti's head as they walked along. 'She is not of your blood, Jhoti – and yet – I hope you do not hate her. She is of Marvinder's blood – and looks so like her, she cannot be denied. She and Ricky took so many photographs of you all and all the places we once knew so well.'

Jhoti smiled as she remembered. A camera was such a novelty in the village – especially a camera like that – large and black with shiny silver lenses. Ricky often had it slung over his shoulders, and wherever he went, flocks of children followed, ready to fall into a perfect group if he should point it in their direction, the little ones positioned to the front, the taller ones behind. And Ricky hadn't stinted. He took so many, thinking with such sensitivity, which images each would want to have as a reminder, as well as which images Beryl would need to live off during the years which would pass until she could next come again.

'They all came to tea, you know: Mrs O'Grady, Kathleen, Michael, Patrick – and even Dr Silbermann who taught Marvinder to play the violin. They came with Beryl and Ricky who were on their way home to America. Only Mr O'Grady didn't come.'

Jhoti could imagine it. Somehow – perhaps from what Marvinder had told her – she imagined the Chadwick house – so big and grand compared to anything they had ever known. She saw a dining-room with a large, round, shining, dark oak table. The photographs would be spread out, covering every inch of the surface, and Jhoti hovered over them, peering intently at each photograph.

'Old Dr Silbermann was so delighted to know that Marvinder continues to play her violin and that she goes to play Beethoven and Mozart sonatas with a retired missionary who had stayed on in Amritsar. Dr Silbermann kept muttering, "She was my angel!" He misses her so much – as we all do.

'But the photos made us weep, Harold and I,' whispered Dora in her ear.

Jhoti knew they would have wept. How could they not, to see the palace and the lake – remembering?

'Thank you for guarding their grave. I saw Edith's face when she looked at the photographs of the graves. She would do anything to have them back – I know it – even though she hated them then. She saw the bond already created between Marvinder and Beryl and realises what she has missed. She will come to you one day, dear Jhoti, I know she will. She will come and make her peace with them.

'But do you know,' Dora laughed unexpectedly, 'I think Edith's in love. She works now, you know. Has a job with a good firm. She has been out a number of times with a young man – one of her colleagues. I think he's her prince. She thinks we don't see – but there's no mistaking the brightness in her eye.'

'Ah yes!' Jhoti sighed and thought of her own daughter; widowed, childless; what future could there be for her? Once she had seen such a brightness in her eye, when a letter had come from that young man. Marvinder called him a boy – like her brother, she had said. But Dora was right. You can't deceive a mother.

Jhoti reached the graveyard. The gate hung open on its rusting hinges. A cow looked up briefly, then resumed its slow cropping of the lean, dry grass. Most of the graves had been stripped of their marble coverings; the statues and headstones had been removed or defaced. Only the grave of the twins was left in its own oasis of remembrance and respect.

Dora hadn't mentioned Jaspal. Well, why should she? thought Jhoti. Ricky had not photographed him. It made him less substantial than the twins. Jaspal! How often in the night she cried out his name.

'Jaspal!' Dora's voice breathed softly. 'Did you think I would forget him. How could I? He went to the very threshold of death with my twins. He is not forgotten. Never. Jaspal will come again – I know it.'

Jhoti began to hum as she approached the grave and laid her posy on the tomb. Another voice joined in; Dora knelt there, as if at their bedside, singing a lullaby. As the song rose and fell, Jhoti tidied up around the tomb, pulling out weeds, clearing away rubble, feeling the peaceful companionship of her friend. Then she lay down beneath the shade of the temple tree and gazed up at the sky hanging through the branches like blue leaves. Her mind was free to soar, but of one thing she was sure; in the end, none of them – Jaspal, Marvinder, the twins – none of them – could escape their karma.

28 The first principal's wife

Evil-doers think, 'No one is looking at us,' but the gods are looking right at them and so is their very own inner Man. The sky, the earth, the waters, the heart, the moon, the sun, fire, Yama and the wind, and night, and the two twilights, and justice know what is done by all who have bodies. **Manu's Law**

The palace was in deep darkness. The kind of darkness associated with desolation and loss; the darkness man and beast experienced before the invention of fire; the darkness of the infinite kind – that can only exist where it is known that somewhere there is light – and in one chamber of the palace, there was light, albeit a single solitary light from a weak electric bulb. It glimmered in a ground-floor room near the main door. This room, which would once have been an ante-room, had a sign on the door saying 'Principal's Office'.

A young woman, sitting behind the great, high, oak desk, a legacy left by the vicar when he returned to England after independence, bent forward into the feeble pool of light and concentrated on the sheets of paper before her. The surface was spread with papers which she shuffled into piles in order of priority. She would not go home till every piece of paper had been dealt with. Her eye scanned a timetable for the next day. A clerk hovered sleepily nearby, waiting for her to release him for the night.

Finally she looked up and rubbed her eyes. 'All right, Gurnam, you may go now.'

'Right, madam.' The clerk respectfully touched his brow and gave a quick bow. Curled up at her feet like a faithful guard dog was Jungli. The clerk stepped over him on the way out. Jungli didn't stir, but watched him from under fluctuating eyebrows which rose and fell.

The woman sighed and carried on working. In the dark-ness of the night a light from a bicycle bobbed down the avenue towards the palace.

Jungli growled in his throat and got to his hands and feet. He arched his back as if all the hairs on his body stood on end.

She listened. She heard the whir of the wheels and the bicycle being kicked into place.

His shadow fell long across the floor and rose slightly up the wall, enveloping her.

The young woman pushed her chair back, surprised. She pulled her veil respectfully over her head and stepped out from behind her desk.

'Father?'

Govind stood in the doorway, partly in shadow, dividing his face like an eclipsing moon.

'Is anything wrong?'

All these years, Govind had never come to the palace. Perhaps it represented everything that had gone wrong in their lives. Now he came secretly in the night as if ashamed.

Govind had worked the land as hard as Marvinder had run the school. Apart from her visits to his home to help Jhoti, they had little contact with each other.

'Will you sit?' she asked, pulling forward a chair.

Govind shook his head. 'What I have to say will not take long.'

Marvinder patted Jungli's head and murmured words of reassurance. Then she folded her hands and waited for her father to continue.

'Now that I have restored the land and it is producing well; now that I have a tractor which does so much of the work, I feel I can leave a man in charge and do what I had always meant to do, and that is use my qualifications. Remember, I have a law degree from London University. I trained as a teacher in London. It had always been my intention to assist Bahadur with the school.'

Govind stopped now and faced his daughter as an equal. 'I know how well the school is doing in your hands and there is a great demand to expand. I have come to offer my services to you. Would you like me to help you with the teaching and running of the college?'

As Marvinder stood half in and half out of the fragile pool of light she felt like a minute speck in eternity. She stood, her feet pressed so hard to the floor, that she was sure she could feel the earth turning beneath her. How strange, she thought, that even when one is most still – almost as still as death – there is always motion. Nothing is still. Nothing stays the same. Everything always changes.

She didn't know how many times her soul circumvented the globe before she raised her eyes to her father and said, 'I know it is something that Bahadur always yearned for.'

Epilogue

Whatever it was, prince's residence or student's college, the palace would always be like a planet, floating in its own universe; never belonging to anyone except itself. Its own memories would be stored in its stones. Events would pass it by; people would come and go – but the palace would exist in its own time and space, relying on the wilderness to close over it from time to time and hide it away. Then it would lie in oblivion, until one day, for the right person, the jungle might part its creepers and weeds and thorns and wild grasses and thick undergrowth, and reveal itself again.

One day a traveller might come again, arriving at dusk in a place he had visited before, to find the person he had loved before.

As before, he might have crossed oceans, covering many miles to return and find that Indian garden, with roses running wild. But this time, if he tried again to pluck a white rose, there would be no roar of a beast to make him flee in terror, but only the throb of crickets in the undergrowth, bats squeaking in the evening air and the warm earth steaming after rain. And if he saw a pale light at the palace, glimmering expectantly, he might turn towards it, wondering if it shone for him, waiting for his arrival.